Bluesman
Outside of Steele (a short horror/thriller in "Tales of
Terror" collection book)

Bluesman

By Christopher S. Allen

Kellan Publishing

Copyright © Christopher S. Allen
Cover Design by Christopher S. Allen
First Kellan Publishing: March 2016

www.kellanpublishing.com
www.bookstore.kellanpublishing.com

Bluesman

By Christopher S. Allen

For Annette Johnson
I haven't forgotten to put roses on your grave.

Chapter 1

I think it's strange what we're allowed to see. We can see stars and galaxies that are millions of miles away and never reach them, yet we know they exist. What we see are the dead. Witnessed but not experienced.

Same as magic, for lack of a better word. Like love, energy, and people, there is good magic and evil magic. S'times it's instilled in a man's bones. Other times, it's adopted and grows like a genetic mutation on the soul.

"Any time you thinkin' evil, you thinkin' 'bout the blues."

Howling Wolf said that.

Evil's what I've been thinkin' lately. Sticky evil. I picture it like sweat from my pores.

I don't consider myself to be from the south, though I come from North Carolina, a good way below the Mason Dixon line, but Granite Falls in Caldwell County, North Carolina isn't my picture of the South. Once I got past Colombia, South Carolina, then I felt I was in the South. Spanish moss adds a lot to the scenery, and is a big part of my perception on how the South should look.

I wasn't born into a very musical family. My grandmother and grandfather are the only ones I know who knew how to play instruments, even if it was only piano and guitar.

I started out like my parents: no real interest in the way of music, other than doing two years of trumpet for the high school marching band.

But then my eyes happened to come across something one day at my grandparent's house. I was examining and looking through some antique stuff in their back room when I accidently placed my hand on something small and triangular. I lifted my hand and saw the guitar pick on a shelf in the roll top desk. It was white and smooth. I picked it up to look at.

Holding it between my thumb, fore, and middle

finger an inch from my nose, the hair and skin on my body prickled and stood up. I also heard a haunting hum. I wasn't sure if it was in my head or all around the room, but I swear I heard what had to be Blind Willie Johnson humming "Dark Was the Night."

Try sleeping after listening to that song at night. Song's a demon taunter if there ever was one; they come out to peer at your soul when it's played.

I swallowed and turned, gently rubbing the pick between my fingers. I swallowed again and placed the pick back. I felt scared and left the room. I went out to the back porch where my grandfather was grilling steaks in the back yard. A few people from church were coming over this evening for a cookout.

He waved at me when he saw me come out. I waved back and went down the steps to the backyard. "Need any help?" I asked when I got near him.

"Not here," he said, turning a steak. "Could do good to get the horseshoes set up."

I nodded and started to walk off.

"E'erything okay?" he asked me. "Look like Old Scratch may been tryin' a bargain with you."

My skin cooled and prickled at the mention of Old Scratch. "Just want to help if I can."

"Okay. Just checking."

I went into the garage and got the horseshoes out and set them up, glancing at my grandfather as he grilled.

When I went back inside, I stayed around my grandmother and helped her in the kitchen. I felt as if I were eight again; afraid to go off alone in the back and upstairs of the house. Strangely, it got better as the day's light started to fade away. But by then, friends and family were here.

Once the conversations, games, and music started, my fear was gone.

Later that evening, my grandfather caught me coming out of the bathroom. "Looking better," he said as I stepped out.

I was about to say something to him but he had already walked past me into the bathroom and closed the door. I went into the kitchen and poured myself a milkshake. I placed the empty blender pitcher in the sink and, as I turned around with my glass to my lips, I saw my grandfather come strolling in. His eyes shined humorously at me.

He looked past me, through the screen door, and then back at me. "Something got to you today," he said. "I'm wondering what *it* was. You didn't do anything wrong earlier, but something spooked you."

I swallowed some of my milkshake and said, "Did I really look scared?"

He laughed. "Scared? Naw. Just... a bit spooked. Like you had a near miss or something."

I took another drink.

"Boy! I bet there is only one thing in this whole house that could do such a thing to a person."

We were in the antique room. My grandfather slid the roll top desk open. My milkshake glass was cold against my hand, but my skin was warm. I wasn't nervous so much now that I was with my grandfather.

"You musta been around this for all of your eighteen years and for some reason it bothered you today." He picked up the ivory looking pick. He looked at the thing curiously, but as if he understood it at the same time. If that guitar pick had any power, my grandfather was in control of it. He placed the pick back on the shelf without offering it to me.

"How'd you come by it?" I asked.

Granddad shook his head. "Your grandmother's daddy had it. I came by it when he passed on."

"I never knew Ne-ma's dad played guitar."

Granddad was nodding. "Wasn't a regular picker, but he picked it up when he was stationed in Mississippi before he was shipped out to the Pacific."

11

"So what's up with it?"

Granddad ran his hands through the sides of his hair before giving me his answer. "Well, it depends what you believe. I'm not quite sure, but I believe the story that was told to me. Whether it's true or not, it still holds something that's beyond mortal man's understanding."

"What were you told about it?"

"Let's get a cup of coffee and sit down in the living room. I can tell you a bit."

My cold glass now replaced with a warm coffee mug, and with my grandfather rocking in his recliner and me on the couch, I listened.

"Well, about that pick, as I was told, it's made from two men's fingers. Your great granddaddy won it in a poker game one night and felt he had been jipped, but he had actually won all the other had. So, anyway, he's shipped out to California with a bit of money and this pick. For some reason, he gets the good idea to buy a guitar before shipping out to Hawaii. There, he plays a bit with other sailors and marines – Hawaiian music – but he's never played before, and he's wanting to play other stuff, darker stuff. On top of that, he claimed his nightmares increased and he had a hard time handling some sort of terror. I think it last his whole deployment. When the war was over and he was blessed to be stationed back in Mississippi, he started to ask around about that pick. Well, sometime he's doing this, someone tells him that it's made from an old blues player's finger. Charley Patton, to be exact.

"The name was familiar to him, but he didn't quite know who Charley Patton was, but your great granddaddy started to listen to some of Charley Patton's music. I'm sure it made him feel a bit odd, but your great granddaddy kept that pick.

"He didn't do much for a while when he was stationed there, but then one night some sailors ask him to come out and play with them, just as a rhythm guitarist.

Your great grandaddy apparently stole the show before the set was over. Didn't even mean to.

"After that show, some guys start asking questions and became a bit violent, saying that they know that guitar pick. Oddly enough, most bluesmen don't even use a pick, but whatever. From a few other shows he ends up doing, a few more people try to get this pick, saying they know of it or something. Your great granddaddy was actually shot at and threatened with a knife over it.

"So with all this concern about one little guitar pick, he looks around and finds someone – I think a gypsy woman or something like that – to do a reading. Before he even brings out the pick she says, "'Welcome, Charlie, Robert; I didn't expect to see you back so soon.'"

"Did he go to the gypsy with a few friends?" I asked.

"No. He went in by his lonesome. The two people she called were the people that made – make – up that pick: Charley Patton and Robert Johnson. One piece of bone from a finger on the right hand, and one piece of bone from a finger on the left hand; musical hands. I think that it was once he learned that, that he quit going out and playing. I think he even retired that pick."

I knew the names, but I was curious why someone would make a pick from their bones – I knew the significance of their hands. I asked.

"Hmm. Well, it comes from various forms of witchcraft and voodoo. You take a piece of the person's soul and essence when you take a part of them. The charm or artifact should bring you some of their skill and luck, about like carrying lucky rabbit's foot."

"Except this gives you the ability to play."

"A little bit, but not everything. Ain't no easy way for anything, and even your great granddaddy had to pick up a few things before he went right to the music, but he got it once he started."

"Because of the pick?"

Granddad shrugged. "I believe it had something to

do with it, but it didn't give him all the ability to play."

Chapter 2

The words stuck with me over the years.

Six years later, that's what I'm seeking. I want to make music. I've acquired the pick and have set off to make my life happen. I get blues halls and small country ramshackle places where I can play, but it ain't what I'm here for. If I can't get a woman, *a woman,* to dance on that floor – any floor – then I'm not doing any good.

Ain't doing no good, as a fella said.

I had 'bout been signed, but another person was picked up in my stead. So, I travel all around the south, mostly east of the Mississippi but I never pass up Louisiana. I'm usually not in the same town every night and I'm occasionally not even in the same state every night.

This morning was rough. I rode a train from Tifton, Georgia to a place about a hundred miles or so outside Vicksburg, Mississippi and walked or hitched the rest of the way. The blues is magical stuff, but you're going to wrestle your demons as well as every other one to actually play and present your magic.

Once I got into Vicksburg, I found the place I'd be playing six hours from now, and went inside. Last time I played the *Bottle* was eight months ago. Management's changed since then, but they know me or my reputation well enough.

"Early," the new owner said, as I sat down at the bar.

I slid my guitar case and pack next to me by the stool. "Got nowhere else to be," I said. "Rye whisky?"

"Early."

I shrugged.

He got a bottle and poured me a double.

"Good stuff," I said.

"When's your band gonna be here?"

"Don't know. Y'all supplied me with one last time. If one ain't ready, I'm sure I could round up a drummer and

15

rhythm guitarist. Hell, maybe just a drummer." I finished my whisky and he filled the empty glass without asking.

"I got a band I can call."

"Nah, nah, man. Call the best drummer, rhythm guitarist, and bassist you can find. Jesus, if you know an organ player, call them too."

"That might be hard to do."

"Yeah, right. Tell 'em *I'm* here, they'll come down. Six hours is plenty of time. Until then, keep up with the doubles."

"Better not be drunk when it's showtime."

"You don't got to worry about that with me."

After my third glass was down, I was given the bottle and I took my guitar to the stage and began to pick at a few songs, my musical charm seeming to hum in my hand as I picked and strummed.

My Baby Tan, which is what I call my guitar, an acoustic Gibson J-45 Custom. I'm sure a lot of people have this guitar, but nobody can make theirs sound like My Baby Tan. Look at Jimmy Page with his Les Paul. Many people have that guitar, but no one makes it sound the way Jimmy does.

I was strumming Howling Wolf's "Back Door Man" and watching some of the people at the bar when the manager came over to me. "Gotcha some players," he said.

I nodded while continuing to strum.

"Drummer, rhythm guitarist, and bassist."

"Talented?"

"Best I know 'round here."

"Well, we'll have this place shaking and may even blow the doors off."

"No rough house."

"You won't get it from me, slim."

He was quiet for a second, and I could tell he was thinking about asking me a question. My bone pick must have distracted him. He watched it as it went up and down my steel strings. "How 'bout a beer, slim? I thought

I spotted some Horny Blonde beer. Fetch a bottle of that."

He left and I turned all my attention back to my music.

I don't drink too, too fast, but I'd gone through two beers and was on my third when I saw my rhythm guitarist headed toward me. *Son of a bitch,* I thought. He was early, by four hours, which didn't bother me, but what did was that I had played with this son of a bitch bastard before, and I couldn't stand him. He was carrying two guitar cases; one electric, one acoustic. He sat them down beside me before addressing me.

"Good to see you again," he said, his eyes and voice without emotion.

"Hello," I said, and I suspect I rolled my eyes.

"What's our set for tonight?"

I pulled a folded piece of paper from my back pocket and handed it to him.

"A lot of these are new. You realize that we'll have to rehearse, don't you?"

I stopped strumming and leaned forward, resting on my guitar, and said. "Of course. It's nothing really; I'll be doing most of the work. You've just got to keep with the drummer keeping up with me. Come on, we'll practice right now." I started to stomp my foot. "Getcha acoustic out."

He did.

"Now, first song, 'Love in an Ink Blot,' I'll open with E minor followed by A minor, followed by B seven, and then I'll go into the notes like so." I started to play. When I stopped I said, "I want you to play this." I started to strum the rhythm. "Now, play with me. See my foot keeping time? Don't need no drummer or nothin'."

I had to do this with him for most of my songs. It pissed me off. The guy wasn't a perfectionist; he was just an idiot who liked to pretend he was smart and talented. When the others came and I showed them the set list and how the songs went, they caught on fast.

"I heard you were about signed," my drummer for tonight said. "Be nice if someone had."

"Don't I know it," I said.

"Who was it they took over you?" the rhythm guitarist, Pain in the Ass, asked.

"Oh, some mediocre kid that looks a bit like a combination of Jim Morrison and Keith Richards."

"Ah, Jareth Richwood. He *is* really good. I had the opportunity to play with him last year. I'm glad Alligator Records picked him up."

I was too busy thinking that if this were the 1930s, he would be shot in cold blood out back.

Despite my problems with the rhythm guitarist, the rest of the show went well. Yet, during the last song, I found myself facing the audience, but my eyes were looking at him as I sang, *"I spit venom/Because I'm the king cobra/I spit venom/Like no man can/I'll strike and drop you for the night/I'll strike and drop you for life…"*

We were paid and I thought about heading out of town right after that, but I opted for another drink and to shake hands and talk with the audience. Doing so meant that Pain in the Ass would talk to me too, once everyone left me alone. I took a drink of beer once an elderly man with white, curly hair had offered me praise and left.

"Where are you headed next?" Pain in the Ass asked me.

"Just someplace down the road."

He nodded, showing no sign of actual concern. "Sounds dangerous. You could stay with me if you like, until you get another show lined up."

"Well, I appreciate that, but I'm a travelling man. I'm more comfortable sleeping under strange, strange skies."

"Okay. Well, just in case," he began, and started writing something down on a napkin with a pen. He slid the napkin over to me and said, "Here's my address and number if you change your mind."

"Thanks," I said, pocketing the napkin and taking

another drink.

He looked at me for a moment longer, expecting me to talk to him, but I kept my eyes forward.

"Well, I better head home," he said. "I've got to be up early. They've got me working this Saturday. I'll be putting in twelve hours."

"I hope you sleep well."

He nodded and walked off. He had both guitar cases in his hands, and I watched him leave through the door. I finished my beer, paid for the last round I had, and left.

Vicksburg is a dead place. The barren south. I walked down streets that looked as if they had just experienced a flood. Every now and then I noticed someone under an awning or outside a door smoking a cigarette. Other than that, it was a quiet night.

I stood beside US-80 looking across the great Mississip'. A train was crossing the bridge to my right. I debated staying on this side of the river or to cross into Louisiana. If I went into Louisiana, I could do well there for a week or more. The first place I'd head for would be Monroe, and I could walk Interstate 20 all the way or hop on one of the trains.

Feeling loose change in my pocket, I took out a quarter and rolled it around in my hand. If I flipped it and it came up heads, then I'd head into Louisiana. I flipped the coin, caught it out of the air, and smacked it down on top of my left hand. George Washington's profile revealed itself in the moonlight. I'd go into Louisiana.

But first I went by a Waffle House and ordered a breakfast platter. I left sometime past one in the morning and made my way down a dirt road to the bank of the Mississippi river. I took out my guitar and started to play. I could probably have played as loudly as I wanted to, but I kept the music soft for the night. I played as I looked up at the sky, at the barges passing on the river, and the trees swaying in the breeze.

"Oh, I'm sleeping under strange, strange skies/Just

another mad, mad day on the road…" I sang.

"Night ballad," a voice said behind me.

I didn't say anything, but continued to play.

"Ain't havin' much success, is we?" It asked. When I didn't respond, I heard the voice cackle. "Hard to get what you's looking for, or maybe you ain't knows whatcha looking for?" That mad laugh again. "I'd say your magic's all run dry. People without part of my finger for a guitar pick have already grown and carried the blues across the country and across the seas. You ain't done commit no acts to secure your place, boy. You got some evil, but you's'n thinkin' you in control o' it." The voice went silent, and I could imagine the entity shaking its head. "Man is *nevah* in control of no evil."

The voice has always hinted at being Robert Johnson or Charley Patton, but has never specified which. Sometimes I think it's both, but over the years I've grown to believe it's neither, and just another demon trying to get me the way it's got others. Despite its lies and twisted words, I suspect that there's some truth to what it says.

"Gonna need new talent. Gonna need *good, new talent!"* Thick and sweet as molasses those words sound with that voice. "You got the sadness and you got the pain, but you ain't done a crime to get you across the plane. That old charm you been usin', it gone, need something new. You gonna need a new Patton/Johnson bone to add to your collection, but who's a new Robert Johnson? Who's a new Charlie Patton?" The voice had moved in front of me, and I could feel warm breath on my face when it spoke. "And you gonna need a young one too. You gonna have to kill a new comer up and take something from their body. But can you expand that pick you been using? Do you have the skill to grow that and to grow the magic you so desperately need?" Mad laughter again. The voice moved to my left. "That's a task you got for yourself. Ain't *neva*h killed a man, ain't *neva*h worked no bone jewelry, and you ain't know a better young talent

20

to kill to get they bones." Again, I sensed this thing shaking its head, if it had one.

Mad laughter erupted, echoing all through the night and across the water. The evil was gone, after about scaring me to death. Its outburst had knocked me on my back, and I doubted I'd be able to sleep tonight, and if I didn't, tomorrow would be a miserable day.

I walked back to the Waffle House. Inside, I tapped on the counter and a once pretty waitress came over, her eyebrows raised to ask, *How can I help you?*

"Do you have a phone I can use?" I asked.

"Yawp. Come over here," she said, and I followed her around to the other side of the counter. She brought a phone out from under the counter and set it before me. Regrettably, I took out the napkin from my back pocket. Pain in the Ass's number was there, so I called him. It rang seven times and he answered on the eighth.

"Hello," his voice said, absent of any emotion. It didn't even sound like he had been sleeping.

"About tonight, it looks as if I'm going to need use of your couch."

"Uh-huh." It was followed by a sigh. "It's past three-thirty in the morning."

"Yeah, I know, but if you unlock the door, I can come in no problem. I'll crash right on your couch. You wouldn't know I'm there until you saw me in the morning."

"I don't like the idea of having my door unlocked." He sighed. "How long will it take you to walk here?"

"I don't know, maybe thirty-minutes, maybe an hour?"

Sigh. "Okay. Where are you?"

"At the Waffle House by the Interstate 20 bridge."

There was another sigh and I thought, *Jesus, buddy, enough with the theatrics.* "I can come get you," he said. "I can be there in fifteen minutes. Next time, just come with me so we don't have to go through all this."

"Thanks," I said. "I'll see you soon."

We hung up.

Fifteen minutes later, I was getting into his passenger seat in the parking lot. He was still in pajamas. I thanked him, but the ride was mostly silent. He lived in a clean one bedroom apartment on Wisconsin Avenue.

"There's the couch," he said, pointing to it when we walked in and he flipped on the light. He moved his finger in front of him, pointing down a small hall, and said, "My bedroom's down there. I'm going back to bed. There's an extra pillow and some sheets in the hall closet by the bathroom." He led me to it and opened the closet door. "You're welcome to them. I'm going to sleep. Goodnight." He walked off and closed the bedroom door behind him. The light emitting from the crack under his door went out.

I grabbed a pillow and sheet and threw them on the couch and turned out the light. I stripped to my boxers and climbed in under the sheet and began to drift off.

A deep laugh rumbled beside me. I opened my eyes and expected to see a smiling face like the Cheshire Cat. I didn't sit up, but moved my eyes around, expecting my demon to speak.

It didn't, and I drifted off into a deep sleep.

* * *

I woke to sunlight streaming through the curtained windows. Without getting up, I looked down the hall and saw that the door to his bedroom was open and knew he was gone for the day. Judging by the sun outside, I deduced that it was probably close to two in the afternoon.

I got up and used the restroom and then went into the kitchen. There were two notes: one on the refrigerator and one between the stove and the sink. The one on the fridge read: *You're welcome to have something, but don't eat me out of house and home. Cups are in the cabinet above the coffee pot. Silverware is in the drawer by the fridge.*

22

I didn't bother to read the one by the sink. I crumpled it up and threw it away and then started fixing myself some breakfast: eggs, bacon, and toast.

With my plate in hand as I ate, I looked around the apartment. Despite his air of being a scumbag, he had an impressive collection of records and CDs. Of course, for musicians fortunate enough to have stable homes, you'll find impressive collections.

I flipped through some of his vinyl. It was a vast collection of artists – old and new – but I focused mostly on blues and rock music. I knew the guy would be the type to keep everything in alphabetical order, yet he kept all the Jack White albums together; the Dead Weather, Raconteurs, the White Stripes, and his solo work. Seeing him, it brought to mind what the voice said last night, about needing a young new talent. Charley Patton died in his forties but Robert Johnson was twenty-seven when he was poisoned, and likely the first member of the twenty-seven club. So I wondered, if I did indeed need another finger or "artifact" for my pick, would I need an established blues guitarist? Or would any do? If any would do, I would go after Jimmy Page, but that wouldn't do. One, he would be too hard to get to, and two, he was too established and had conquered what he had set out to do. I needed someone still on the rise but close to breaking *in*.

Jareth Richland, a worthy adversary, and one who got something before me, would be poetic to murder and then incorporate one of his bones to my magic pick, but he has five years or more to go before he'll do anything poetically or musically worthwhile. No, Jareth Richland was signed for looks and stage performance; important stuff, but something that should always come after talent.

He was out. I needed someone who was like me that could be sacrificed, and I could use their talent and energy for my own gain.

I still had a bit of egg on my plate and some bacon. I

took a bite of egg and found that Pain in the Ass had the Trogg's *Love is All Around* album and put it on. I turned it all the way up and continued to flip through the albums. Evil was on my mind. And since the mind was feeling dirty, I decided that my body should be cleaned. I left the vinyl collection and took a shower.

Naked, with the exception of a towel wrapped around my waist, I returned to the vinyl. The Troggs were spinning, but putting out no music. "Catch Hell Blues" was ringing in my head, so I went for the White Stripes, but then my hand stopped just over the album and hovered. Next to my main choice was a Whitley Jones album, a fairly new blues singer whose voice reminded me of Billie Holiday or Melva Houston.

I took Whitley over the White Stripes.

Her sax player 'bout burst my eardrums on the opening song. It was quickly followed by Whitley's high wail and then the main riff and drums. As the song played, I went over to Pain in the Ass's bookshelf and examined his taste in books. It wasn't tasteful.

The guitar's intro to the second song spun me around. I stared at the spinning record as if I expected the guitarist to be there. I went over to the album sleeve and flipped it over to the back where all six band members stood with their instruments (or drum sticks) in front of an old wooden building with grass up to their shins. I read over the names of the members. The guitarist's name was Sonny Nolans, no doubt a stage name, the name Nolans a nod to the dialect of saying N' O'le'ns.

And Sonny Nolans looked young. No older than twenty-five, if that. The way he was dressed and held himself in the picture reminded me of a young Big Bill Broonzy.

"Some'n' tell me you foun' your next artifact," the demon's voice said under the sound of Sonny Nolan's guitar.

I unconsciously nodded in agreement.

"Now you gone have ta find 'im an' kill 'im!" The thing's mad laughter rang off the walls. It fit with Whitley's song.

Chapter 3

Whitley's self-titled album was released last year. Once, in Memphis, I'd played a club before she and her band went on, but I didn't stick around to meet them or to listen to them. Hearing her album, I wish I had stayed to see the live performance.

I looked around for a computer and found one in Pain in the Ass's room. I was surprised to see his laptop open and not requiring a password once I shook the screensaver away. I got online and looked up Whitley Jones to see if she was touring. Luckily for me she was. Tomorrow she would be performing in Phoenix, Arizona and remain out west for another week, but then she would be in Baton Rouge the week after for a concert.

I didn't like the idea of sticking around Louisiana that long, but it had enough towns and bars to keep me occupied until I needed to meet Sonny Nolans in Baton Rouge.

The phone by the kitchen bar started to ring. I didn't answer it. When the phone quieted it instantly started to ring again, so I picked up. It was Pain in the Ass.

"Hey, it's me," he said.

"Hello."

"I wasn't sure if I would catch you. When do you plan to leave?"

"Uh… I planned for some time today. Probably at sundown."

"Okay, well I'll be home in about three hours. I have some barbecue chicken marinating in the fridge, put it on at seven. Can you cook?"

I rolled my eyes. "I can and do often."

"Good. I've got some crawfish and corn that you can boil too. Also some fresh garden green beans in the pantry. I should be back at eight-thirty or nine. See you then, and thanks," he said. I heard a click, followed shortly by dial tone.

I liked how he had given orders, no asking, and ended it all with a thanks. At least he had some manners.

Pain in the Ass's washer and dryer were in the bathroom. I put what few clothes I had in the wash and then went back to the bookshelf to see if I could find at least one book worth reading.

There was one. *Essentials of Geology (Fourth Edition)*. Likely a left over from his college years. I read that until I heard the washer stop and then dog-eared my current page and threw it on top of my guitar case. I put my damp clothes in the dryer, started it, and returned to my book. When my clothes were ready, I changed into them and wondered what I would do next. I knew a wholesale tobacco outlet was near here, maybe a fifteen to thirty minute walk from the apartment. A good cigar's a rare luxury when you're on the road, and the outlet would likely be closed when I set out tonight for Louisiana, so I left the apartment for my cigars. When I got back, I would have to immediately start on dinner, and I would still probably not have it ready when Pain in the Ass got in.

* * *

I got back later than I expected, but I still had a little over an hour to get everything ready. It occurred to me that perhaps I should have fixed this earlier, eaten my fill, and set out; get my cigar and journey to Louisiana.

But *c'est la vie*, as a wise musician once put it.

Pain in the ass arrived about the time he said he would. Some of the food had about twenty minutes left to cook. I said it'd be a bit; he just nodded and started to set the small table by the kitchen entrance.

I stayed for another hour after we ate. Before leaving, I asked if there was a bit of food I could take, just something to have in the morning. He gave me an open box of apple crisp protein bars. Three behemoth bars remained inside. I was surprised he parted with them easily and didn't complain when dinner wasn't ready as soon as he got in. Maybe beneath that arrogant exterior there was a somewhat decent person.

I left and went to a railway bridge that crossed the Mississippi and boarded an empty boxcar that was rolling down the track.

Since I was going to be in Louisiana for a while, I decided that once I got to Monroe I would get a room for the night and probably the next day. From there, I could call a few people I'd played with in the past and get a small band together. Once I had a band, I'd call some clubs and bars that would book us.

I slept on the train until it stopped in Monroe. A few bums had ridden in a boxcar ahead of mine and we entered Monroe as separately as we had come in. About the only difference was that I had money and could afford a decent place to stay.

I got a room at the Motel 6 for fifty bucks a night. I only planned to stay for two nights, if that. I lay on the bed and dozed for about thirty minutes. When I woke, I rummaged through my pack and found my notepad that had a list of the contacts I'd met worth keeping in touch with. Most were musicians, but I also had fans, bar and club owners, and anyone worth knowing. I flipped to the owner of *Bar 3*. It was a place that played mostly shit music: techno, rap, and other brain damage. But Sule, the owner, liked my playing so much that he was willing to do just about anything to get me in to play.

"Hey, hey, Sule," I said.

"Who the hell's this?" he asked, unamused.

"The best damn blues singer and player in the South. The one you're willing to do just about anything for."

"Oh, oh! Hey, how you doin'? Gonna be around Monroe anytime soon?"

"As a matter of fact, I'm in Monroe right now."

"Say word, boy, how long you around for? Whatcha got lined up?"

"One or two things," I lied. "What nights have you got open that I could come perform?"

"Hell, it's a bit sudden, but I should be able to get you next weekend."

"Next Thursday and Friday. It's also negotiable depending on who else is hiring and what they're paying. Every venue I play, nine times out of ten, it's standing room only."

"Hey, man, this is the place for you. I'll make it happen and we'll have those nights sold out the door."

Somewhere in my room I heard the demon's soft baritone laughter. My eyes darted around before I spoke to Sule. "If the price is right, we'll be there."

I hung up, made some other calls and started putting a band together. It became a night of business for me, making all the arrangements I could, most importantly, making sure to get booked to open as a special guest for Whitley and her band when they played in Baton Rouge.

* * *

I've got a knack for putting bands together, and we opened every venue with Elmore James's "Dust My Broom" and then went into my original songs, sometimes playing a different variation of them. We played the *Bar 3* for two nights and did two other nights at *Live Oaks Bar and Ballroom* before leaving Monroe for a few other happening Louisiana cities for a week long traveling escapade of blues.

The short lived tour ended in Lafayette. What a night that was.

It started out great. Baby, that whole performance was great. But darkness has a way of getting into people, and darkness is always with me.

Some redneck, blue collar-low-class-camo cap-Budlight drunk kept trying to get to my microphone between two songs. I didn't mind it the first time; someone really enjoying the music, wanting to give a shoutout. But the second time, keep your distance from me; you ain't the show.

And perhaps he thought I was challenging him when I sang, *"I spit venom/Because I'm the king cobra/I spit venom/Like no man can/I'll strike and drop you for the night/I'll strike and drop you for life…"*

Again, I was looking at an enemy when I vented my anger and my personal venom through song. When we finished that song, my bassist began to thank the audience and give some stories about the tour. Before he could end with a laugh, the drunken asshole came on stage again.

I smacked him in the face with the bottom of my guitar. Nose gushing, he fell off the stage, landing on a few other drunks whilst crashing into a table; a situation that would typically be followed by silence or an immediate fight, but I hammered out a high intro similar to an Elmore James riff, and created a new song on the spot. *"Get back, Jack/There will always be more holes in the ground/That's where you belong/Safe and sound/I said safe and sound…"*

The band managed to keep up.

Outside, four in the morning, we loaded up the van. It belonged to the drummer and we had spent a few cramped nights in it or outside of it on the ground as we toured around Louisiana.

"Good tour, buddy," the drummer said to me. "Need to do a longer one, cover more ground."

"My life's one big tour," I said. "But I know what you're saying."

He nodded to me. "I'm thinking 'bout heading up to Nashville. See if I can get some promising work as a session musician. Not much worth doing down here."

"Whaaat?" said our keyboard player. "You know they don't consider drummers to be musicians."

"Oh shut up," said the drummer.

"You guys take care," I said, laughing and slamming

the back shut. "I'll be in touch next time I pass through ol' Louie."

"Where are you headed now?"

I shrugged. *Straight across 10 to Baton Rouge.* "Everywhere between here and Savannah and back again."

They laughed and shook their heads. "Must be some life," said the rhythm guitarist, hanging out by the passenger door.

"Some life," I said.

The others nodded and remained silent. The drummer broke it by saying, "Come on guys, we got a long haul to get back to Monroe." To me he said, "We'll be seeing you." They piled in and I watched the van drive up the gravel road and then turn onto the street and out of my life.

Reggie's River Joint had a deck that wrapped around the place, and the back part actually had a swing. The sky was cloudy and I expected rain, so I went up the steps and set my pack and guitar case under the swing and spread out on it, gently rocking. The swing wasn't soft, but I was so beat, that I bet I could have fallen asleep on it in seconds.

Except...

Something hard hit me in the forehead. My hand shot to cover my wound and I toppled over onto the deck. I felt a stone under my ribs and realized it had been thrown at me.

Another one rattled off the wooden side of the building and landed on the deck. I kept my head covered with my hands.

It was quiet. I listened for more rocks. I listened for the sound of a person. I listened for the sound of a demon.

Silence.

Then...

The sound of boots on mud and gravel. They were cautiously approaching. Soon they would be on the steps.

31

It was dark, but good eyes could spot my movement through the rafters if I decided to sneak away.

The creak of a board.

Too late for me to run; I would have to fight.

Quietly, I grabbed the handle on my guitar case and slowly inched it to me. When I saw the shadowy outline, about five feet from me, I thrust the neck of my guitar case into their crotch and tried to force them down the steps. They groaned in pain and buckled forward but did not fall. I stood and went to hit them with the case, but they hit me in the side of the head with a rock, about an inch from my temple. I about lost balance.

I tossed my case at my assailant, knocking him down the steps. He landed on his back and I saw that he was redneck-Budlight drunk. He tried to get to his feet and I went to jump on him, but he rolled out of the way and got up into an attack stance and landed two hits on me before I could see where he'd gotten.

Another blow came on the back of my head and dropped me to the ground. I scrambled to my case, got a hand on it, and used it as a weapon once more, hitting the redneck in the ribs. The latches opened and my guitar and loose papers fell out.

The redneck stumbled, kept balance, and picked up my guitar by the neck and wielded it like an axe. He swung at me twice. I ducked both swings, and charged him on the second attack, tackling him to the ground. I tried to be mindful of my Baby Tan, but she snapped when we hit the ground.

"Gone need *KILL* this honky!" the demon's voice yelled. It was followed by its mad laughter. "Gone need be a killin' this mo'nin'. Yes suh, a killin' this mo'nin'!"

I picked up my crumpled Baby Tan by the neck and brought the body down on the redneck's face. She broke and her strings whipped around wildly, like mad prisoners now free from their tension.

"Gone need to be killin' this honky! Can you say

hallelujah?! Another soul for me, yes suh, soon to be!"

I grabbed the loose strings, still attached to the bridge, and wrapped them around the redneck's throat, choking him.

The demon continued to singsong as the redneck and I struggled on the damp ground. His body shook on top of mine. I kept pulling the strings tighter and tighter. Several times I thought I would cut through his carotid artery.

Then the body was still. No nerves convulsing, no lungs a breathing.

I was sure he was dead, but I kept the strings pulled taut around his throat for a couple more minutes. Once I was sure he was dead, I looked for my Johnson/Patton pick. I was more panicked about losing it than I was when being attacked. I found my charm by the guitar case and offered up a small prayer of thanks when I felt the smooth bone hum between my fingers. I held it in my right hand and lightly pet it with my left, enjoying its smoothness and its magic power.

I rolled the dead body down to the river and pushed him in. Warm body like this, the gators would hopefully get to him soon.

I picked up the pieces of my guitar and loose papers and put them back in the case. I checked the murder site for more evidence. It looked like I got it all. When I got to the porch, I threw the rock that had hit me and drawn blood into the river, picked up my pack, and set off for Interstate 10.

It was muggy now and a light drizzle fell. By ten in the morning, it would be a skin sticky trek.

The demon spoke to me until dawn. Just before the sun broke the darkness, the demon said, "Yous'n soul gettin' rich now, yes suh. Yous'n body was gettin' rich, but not your soul. Your *man* body, hmph, but takin' that life making you richer. Mmhmm, yous'n take my woid for it. You had you a real struggle, now you got something hard behind you and something hard ahead of you. Gettin' rich, gettin' rich." Then it was gone, just as the sun began to turn the sky red and gold.

Chapter 4

I reached the town of Henderson about fifteen past noon, feeling a minute past dead. Henderson's a small place by Lake Bigeaux. You're in and then you're out of it before you see it go by. I've passed through several times in my travels, but never became close with anyone. There was one place I liked: Pat's Fisherman Wharf Restaurant. If my guitar was intact, I could probably play for a few tips. But I was beat and hungry. I took a table on the deck that allowed me to face the water. I ordered four beers, some boudin, and a cup of seafood gumbo. The beers came first and I downed them.

Food came. I ate. Ordered more beer.

I drank one and fell asleep in my chair, head back, resting against the building. They let me sleep for an hour before waking me. I paid for what I ordered so they could see I had money and wasn't a bum. I ordered another beer and told them if I drifted off again to leave me; I just wanted to rest in the shade and listen to the lake life.

I woke to the owner tapping my foot with his. The sun was in the west and I figured the time was around six o'clock. I was surprised they let me nap for so long. "Son," the owner started, "we've got an inn if you'd like to stay for the night."

"How much?"

"Seventy-seven dollars a night."

I nodded and said, "I'll take it, but I'm going to stay here a bit. Have another drink or two." He left. I spent another hour on the deck and then got a room for the night. I left for Baton Rouge at ten the next morning. My only stop was Rosedale, where I bought some bottles of water at a gas station. An hour and a half later, I was crossing into Baton Rouge.

First thing first, I needed a new guitar. I regretted it, but I had to lose my Baby Tan. Broken she may be, but so much had come from her. I went to a dumpster behind

Applebee's and lifted one of its lids. I kissed Baby Tan goodbye on her headstock and dropped her into the filth.

I kept the case and all my contents within. I stopped by a Guitar Center and viewed what they had for sale. A Gretsch G9555 New Yorker with a pickup caught my eye. I asked to play it. A worker got it down for me and I played one of my own songs. When I bought it, the guy knocked $150 off for my autograph.

Now, outside in the sun, I wondered what to do. I had a while yet before I needed to head to this concert and open as a special guest. I walked in the sunshine, headed toward LSU. I had played there maybe three years ago for ten thousand dollars. Now, I just wanted to head to the lake and play my guitar and get a woman.

I passed under the dorms and heard music coming through open windows. A lot of it I didn't like or even listen to, but I did hear "Hats off to Roy Harper," which sent Plant's voice and Page's guitar vibrating through the air. Hearing Zeppelin put me in a pleasant mood, the kind I needed for playing on a sunny afternoon.

A good many people were out by the lake. Students, by the look of them, grilling, jogging, and a group of girls in bikinis sunbathing. I sat under the shade of a willow tree, my back against the trunk and my new Gretsch in the crook of my right leg and hip. I tuned it and started to play softly. I sang one of my songs and then started to play Tracy Chapman's "One Reason" and got a bit louder. Everyone loves that intro and so I knew I had their attention.

When I finished the song, one of the students called out, "Hey! You played here before."

"That's right, schoolboy, and I just came into town."

"Want a burger?"

"And a beer, if you got it."

He waved me over. I took a can of Coors from the cooler, popped it, and had a drink. The kid (though he was likely two years younger than me) brought a burger over on a Dixie plate.

"You playing at the University?" he asked after I took a bite.

"Nope. Doing a special open for Whitley's group tonight. We'll be at the Varsity Theater." I turned to face a blond looking up at me from her towel. "I bet you'd look good on the dance floor," I said to her. "You with that coffee and cream tan you've worked on."

She blushed at the attention I'd given her.

"Have you got tickets?" I asked.

"No. I – I'm afraid I don't know much about who's playing."

"Well, it's not a problem. I can get you in backstage and you can meet everyone."

She lowered her Ray Bans to the end of her nose. I could see her eyes, deep blues, and they were giving me the look that put the Elvis wiggles in my knees. She pushed her shades up and the tip of her tongue emerged and wetted her lips. Her friends were watching me too: two brunettes, another blond, and a redhead. Out of all of them, the redhead seemed the least interested in me. The others watched as I talked to their friend, but the redhead was content to lie on her back and face the sunny sky.

A few other guys came by and tried to make conversation with me. I humored them and had another beer.

I finished the beer and looked to Coffee and Cream, who now stood next to me. I came close to putting my hand around her waist, but I wanted us to keep with the teasing until we left. One of the dudes asked me a question as I tossed the empty can into a trash bag, but I ignored him and looked at Coffee and Cream and said to her, "It's about that time. Gonna need to head out soon and get setup at the Varsity."

"Oh, okay. Let me get my things." She started to roll up her towel.

I put my guitar in its case, and then we started down

37

a cement path. "We'll have to head back to my dorm," she said, "I need to change. My roommates shouldn't be there, so you'll be okay to come in."

"Sounds good to me."

She took her keys out when we neared the parking lot. "Did you drive?" she asked.

"Nope."

"Okay, well I'm this Jeep here."

Her Jeep was a black Wrangler with the top off. I put my guitar and pack in the backseat and got up front. Coffee and Cream threw her towel and clothes in the back and then got in and started the Wrangler.

It was a five minute drive from here to the Miller Hall parking lot, and it was about the same time from the parking lot to her dorm room. She was right about her mates being out, and once the door closed, Coffee and Cream's top fell to the floor, revealing a thin line of white on her back. She turned and I saw her beautiful half tan breasts.

"How long do we have?" she asked.

"An hour, maybe two."

Her bottoms fell to the floor and she stepped out of them. She took a step toward me, then turned away and walked to her drawer and began to rummage through it.

"Whatcha lookin' for?" I asked.

"I'm seeing what clothes I have that'd be good for tonight."

I dropped my pack on her desk chair and rested my guitar against the desk and sat on the bed and said, "There'll be time for that later. Why don't you come over here, let me have a look at you."

She stopped what she was doing and pushed the drawer shut. She walked over and stood before me. I placed my hands on her waist and pulled her close, breathing in the sweet smell of her tanning oil, and I kissed her just below the navel.

Her hands ran through my hair, and then she

unbuckled my belt and slid my pants down to my shoes. I kicked them off and she removed my boxers while I simultaneously took off my shirt. Her head bent and I felt the warmth of her mouth slide over my shaft. When she rose, there was a condom on my erection. I didn't see her get one out, but how she worked it was a decent surprise.

I pulled her on top of me.

We did it twice, with something of a rest in between. During that time I played her a few of my songs.

After our last roll, she took a shower. I dressed and thought of my strategy for tonight. I debated about leaving Coffee and Cream behind and walking to the Varsity Theater; it was only ten minutes away.

Then she walked in. Wet, tan, and now naked with a damp towel at her feet. When opportunity knocks, especially twice, take it, even if it's murder.

I had her three times within an hour. Seemed like a good omen to me.

We got to the Varsity Theater at a little past six. I wouldn't go on until eight. They expected Whitley to arrive at any time for sound checks. Everything was set up, so I tested my Gretsch and voice on their equipment. I did that for about forty-five minutes or more. They told me that Whitley had arrived and that my sound was good. I set my guitar aside and left the stage. Coffee and Cream was in the back at the bar. I joined her and ordered myself a beer and her another Porch Crawler.

The beer came first and I asked the bartender if there was a place that would deliver something to eat, preferably gumbo. He told me that I should go backstage, that they were probably taking orders if anyone wanted something before show time.

Someone was sitting on a stool beside me, before I saw him, I heard him say, "Just tell me. I'm getting ready to head back." Then to the bartender he said, "Sir, I need to trouble you for two gin and tonics, two beers, and one double Irish."

I looked to see who was beside me.

There stood Sonny Nolans. Wearing a summer straw hat, plaid shirt, and blue cotton pants, he continued talking before noticing me, saying, "Just hand me a Negra Modelo – please – before taking the rest backstage." Sonny looked at me, and the realization of who he was seeing rearranged his face. Sonny's eyes grew wide and he reminded me of someone going sober in the presence of a cop or their parents. "I can't believe it," he said. "I didn't realize who you were." He put out his hand and I shook it. "Sonny Nolans," he said.

"Nice to meet you," said I.

The bartender set Sonny's beer down before him. Sonny took a drink. "Whew. I figured you were a roadie." He pointed his finger at me, bobbing it up and down and said, "I thought I heard one of your songs playing out here."

I smiled.

"Listen, what was it you wanted? I got to head back there. Don't want to keep Whitley waiting."

I started to speak, but the demon spoke first, saying, "Ohhhh-ooh! Ain't this something! He' you got yo artifac'. Boy! Righ' befo' you! How's you gonna do it? Poison? Stabbing? Shooting? Hell, you ain't got no gun. Gonna have 'a be quiet in your killing."

After what seemed like a minute, I said, "Just some gumbo. All I'm really in the mood for, Sonny. Thanks."

"Okay, buddy. I got it." Sonny took a drink. "Say, you want to play a few songs together during our set?"

"Sure. What have you got in mind?"

"Well, I'll let Ms. Whitely know, but I figured our faster, bluesier stuff. Something in the middle or near the end of our set. 'Broke Down Car Blues', 'Early Flight Relations', Whisky Over Water', and that kind of stuff."

"Fine by me. Let me know what songs you want me on, and I'll be there."

"All right. Well, I'm going to head backstage and be

sure to get them your order. See you in a bit." He took his beer and left.

"*AHHHH-HAHAHAHA!*" That demon voice that only I could hear boomed. "He gone play with his own worst enemy! Don' even know it. You's a legen', ohhhh, yes he know that, but he don' know your alterative motive! HA!"

"Enough," I grumbled.

"What, baby?" Coffee and Cream asked.

"Nothing," I said. "I need to get with 'em. You should come back in about ten minutes."

"Okay."

I stood and went backstage. Everyone was moving about. I went back just as Whitley's band went out to check their instruments. The demon was silent. I listened to them play while I sat on a box and waited.

When our food arrived I had about ten minutes to eat before I went on. I took my time eating and opened twenty minutes after I was scheduled to. An announcer went on and said, "We have a very special guest tonight. He's known as the Traveler of the South, and he is here to open for you!"

A rush of applause erupted as the announcer walked away. I took the stage and said, "Good evening." Then I immediately went into a song. It was a darker and slower song of mine. Bluesy, but it border lined rock. "*The voice/The one that always speaks to me/In the dead of night/In that darkness/I don't want to see/Take the night/Wrap it around me/Oh that voice/Always beckons me/The voice…*"

I played for an hour or more and then welcomed Whitley Jones to the stage. I whispered in her ear and she kissed my cheek. I went backstage and immediately locked lips with Coffee and Cream.

Whitley Jones and her band played for over an hour and a half before I came out to play with them. God, was that a blast! Sonny Nolans came up beside me and played with me and against me. He was a true talent.

41

Playing an encore with them, especially Sonny, was one of the hardest things I've ever done.

I talked to them backstage, but I put a lot of attention on Sonny Nolans.

"Who influenced you the most?" I asked him.

"Who influenced you?" he retorted. A big grin came across his face.

"I asked you first."

The grin grew. This was a man who was genuinely happy to be alive and wouldn't want to do anything else. "Jimi Hendrix with 'Hey Joe' and Jimi in general. That's what got me to pick up the guitar. Now, who influenced you?"

"Robert Johnson set me on the path. Mississippi Fred McDowel is the one who's influenced my style."

He made a puzzled face and said, "Funny, you don't use a slide much in your playing."

"Well, I had a slide but I recently lost it. Didn't realize it was gone until tonight."

"Should have let me know, man, I could have let you borrow mine."

I kind of shrugged and said, "No big deal." Then added, "Where are you headed after this?"

"We'll be in Charlotte next Friday, Nashville after that. Then the weekend after that we'll be in Pittsburgh and then New York."

"Cool. But I meant what are you doing later on tonight?"

"Oh-h. I don't know. We're not really big on the party scene."

"Yeah, but the night's young. I'll be gone in the morning or sometime tomorrow. Anyway, I'm sure we can find some place or places worth going to. After I played at LSU a few years ago, we went to the Penthouse Club afterward. I think we stayed all night, but I'm up for bar hopping if you'd rather do that." I looked at Coffee and Cream. "You up for a night of fun?" I asked her.

"Oh, totally," she said. "I'm always up for a fun time."

"So whatcha say, Sonny, ready to shake 'em on down?"

He finished his beer and said, "Eh, why not?"

I heard Whitley make a motherly *ahem* sound. "You fools can do what you want to, but I'm not gonna go with ya'll."

"Oh, come on, Missy Whitley Jones," said Sonny. "You always enjoy a night out after a concert."

"Tonight ain't the night, but ya'll go on ahead. Except I don't want nobody callin' me at sunrise to pick your drunk, sick asses up, you understand me?"

"Yes ma'am."

I left with Coffee and Cream and Sonny Nolans. We were in her jeep; me beside her and Sonny in the back along with my guitar and pack. The drummer and bassist were going out with us, but they were getting a ride to the club some other way.

I was an asshole on the ride over. Not verbally or anything, but I was one just the same. Sonny was talking to Coffee and Cream. I can't remember the whole conversation, but I believe it was about touring. Anyway, I had a case of Coffee and Cream's CDs on my lap. She had a lot of bad music, and any Lil Wayne CD I saw or Green Day or Fall Out Boy or 2 Chainz, I threw it right out. She didn't see me either. Sonny may have, but he didn't say anything about it.

We arrived at the Penthouse Club.

I was walking toward the club when Sonny called out, "Yo! You worried about, you know," he said, gesturing with his head to the rear of the jeep.

"Nothing to worry about," I said, and waved him over. I had one encounter where my guitar and pick were stolen, for all of a minute, then the thief dropped dead. Probably from fear or from the touch of the demon. Nothing interfered with my destiny and got away with it.

All the girls were painted up tonight. Naked except for g-strings and paint; they reminded me of the Pink Floyd women with the album covers painted on their nude backs. The purple, blue, and neon green light hit the women carrying trays of champagne and gin and gave them a psychedelic glow.

We walked around a crowd at the round stage, where two painted women pole danced while a woman twirled fire between them, and took a seat at a round table. Coffee and Cream sat on my lap and Sonny Nolans sat across from us. Three chairs remained open. Out of the corner of my eye, I thought I spotted a large black snake in an empty chair. *"Tsss, tsss,"* went the demon's sound. *"Ain't got no poison… Best get Sonny liquored up and lead him out the back do', an' takes his life. An' then get a knife or stone, and takes his bones."* The demon cackled before I saw the snake dissipate in thin traces of black fog.

"What's the matter?" Sonny asked. "See something you don't like?"

I turned my head to look at him. "Something like that," I said.

A young beauty, painted up as if she were a part of some hoodoo ritual, came by and took our drink order. The other drummer and bassist found us about five minutes after she left, but they already had drinks of their own in hand. The two sat down at opposite ends of the table.

We didn't talk to one another at first as we were too focused on the painted girls and their performances. Coffee and Cream spoke though, whispering all the sexual things she wanted to do to me. She knew how to work a man.

Our drinks came and I instantly ordered more. I played it like that: encouraging everyone to down theirs while I kept ordering. A couple of mine I gave to Coffee and Cream so I wouldn't get drunk. I stopped giving them to her when she passed out on top of me.

"We, we, we going to party all over tonight?" the bassist asked.

I nodded and said, "All night long." Then added, "What's your name again?"

"Steve."

"Bassist Steve," I said, thinking the name over. I looked at Sonny. He had had his chin on his chest for a moment, but he quickly snapped his head up right and blinked his eyes.

"Whew!" Sonny exclaimed. Almost on que, a mint julep was placed before him. "God!" Sonny went on, "We going anywhere else?" A nude painted girl walked by and Sonny followed her with his gaze. "I don't see any reason why we should go anywhere else. Hell, I doubt I'll be able to walk out of here."

"Drink your drink," I said, and took a sip of my spiced rum.

I watched Sonny as he drank, thinking of how I'd get his hand as an artifact. I couldn't risk getting too blitzed tonight; I had to do this murder and then get out of this city without passing out a mile or two down the road. Getting picked up by the police, who would happen to find a bloody hand in my guitar case, is not an outcome I'd take after all this effort.

No, no. I'd have to be careful. All of us leave together. Somewhere down the road the others would have to fall out, leaving me with Sonny. Once alone, I'd push him off the mortal coil.

I dismissed myself and used the restroom. I was at the urinal for less than a minute, then my old fiendish observer started to speak.

"Night'ssss going deeper," it droned, seeming to grow louder. "Night'ssss gonna go till it's gone! Ain't no artifact till you act!"

I hammered the plunger with the palm of my hand and left the restroom. The demon's cackling followed behind me.

Sonny Nolans had managed to get one of the painted girls onto his lap and his lips were, I'm sure, too close to her neck for HR purposes. It didn't bother me, and I hoped, if Sonny could be so lucky, that he'd get laid tonight before I took his life.

Whatever Sonny was telling her, she seemed to be quite taken with it.

"What time do you get off, doll?" I asked her, taking a seat.

The smile Sonny had brought to her lips dropped at my question. "'Till close, baby," she said.

I tilted my head and said, "Ain't got time for that. Sonny, if you're looking for a lay, I'll get you one at the Texas Club. I've played there and they owe me." I stood up and brought Coffee and Cream to her feet. "Come on, this place ain't Chuck Berry enough for me."

I didn't tell a lie but I didn't tell the truth. I got Sonny a woman when we got to the Texas Club but she was teasing him more than anything else. I had to drive us there and I left Coffee and Cream passed out in the jeep.

Here, I was able to drink a bit more, and the people that worked the *Texas Club* expected me to. The drummer stayed with us but the bassist, Steve, retired for the night. These two fools were drunk, and any conversation they or anyone else tried to start with me was only a distraction. I eyed Sonny, trying to figure out how to get Sonny's hand. Maybe both, now that I looked at them, running smoothly over a blonde's skin.

I took a sip of rye whisky, then decided to finish off the glass.

"Another on the house," the bartender said, snatching up the empty glass.

I looked around at everyone out on the floor. I was bored and my mind was too bogged to enjoy being out. All I could agree on was that the band playing sucked.

Another drink was placed before me.

Too long a night, too long a night, I thought.

I had a goal that no one else had. Also, it was too dark for most people, even by today's standards.

"Wha's a matter?" Sonny called to me.

"Bad music," I said.

"Ain't that bad. Anyway, this one wants a better look at the band."

"I want to dance," the woman said, looking offended.

"That too," said Sonny.

The woman grabbed him by the arm and pulled Sonny out into the brouhaha.

They disappeared from my sight, but I knew that I hadn't lost Sonny for the night. Not yet at least.

I took a drink and finished it off. As I lowered the glass from my lips, it slipped from my fingers and shattered on the floor. I stared at it and then picked up a three inch shard. I had a weapon. I looked around and realized that no one had seen me drop the glass. Hand by my leg, I gently ran my fingers over the glass shard. It was sharp with a prominent point.

"Someone taken care of your order?" a bartender asked me.

"No. I'm not having anymore."

He nodded and went to tend someone else.

A few minutes later the drummer found me. He was soused and wanted to leave. I helped him to the jeep and dropped him in the backseat, away from my pack and guitar.

Back inside, I returned to my spot and stood next to my stool, back against the bar, watching the crowd. My foot crunched on the broken glass whenever I moved.

Finally, Sonny came stumbling out of the crowd. He still had the woman with him.

"I think you should drop the weight," I said to Sonny, when the woman had turned her head.

A questioning look came across his face. "Whatcha mean?" he asked.

"Well, your drummer has already passed out. I had

47

to get him in the jeep. I think it's time we head out."

"Go ahead, man. I'll head back with this one. Listen, it was nice to meet you and damn good to play with you."

"Sonny, I'm not going just yet." *Was hoping you would be.*

"All right, well, suit yourself."

His woman broke away from him and ordered a drink.

"You sure she's taking you with her tonight?"

"I don't know what else she'd be doing."

I nodded. "Well, she's got the right idea right now; I'm going to get a drink." I bumped in beside her and ordered a Horny Blonde beer. Sonny's sugar gave me a look. "It's a beer, Sweet," I explained to her. "Though I got another outside. She's not as hopped up as this beer will be," I said with a wink.

Her cocktail and my beer were placed before us. She grabbed her drink and started to walk away. I stopped her and said, "Don't lead Sonny on too much. He's got a show tomorrow and we'll be leaving shortly after dawn. Best to wrap things up."

"If it's not too much trouble, could I come back with you guys?"

No. "Yeah, but the ride over may be a little crowded."

It didn't matter. She went to Sonny and told him that she was ready to leave. She had come with her friends and texted them that she was leaving. Once they were in the back of the Wrangler, I started the jeep and drove off. As I made my way down the street, I thought of what I needed to do. Sonny was drunk enough to be an easy kill but the woman... She wasn't too far gone. And it would be hard to get her away from Sonny.

They started going at it in the backseat. Not screwing or anything, as far as I could tell, but making out heavily. I would glance at them in the rearview as I drove. Sonny looked to be close to passing out, but his woman was revved up and kept at him.

I took the opportunity to drive out of Baton Rouge. Heading north, the Mississippi always somewhere to my left, even if it was out of sight.

The woman started to moan in the backseat. At least she was distracted. I was afraid that she or Sonny would notice that we weren't surrounded by city lights anymore. I took a side road, knowing that the time to act was quickly approaching.

I was coming up to a bridge over a bayou. I looked in the rearview at my passengers. The woman was still atop Sonny, but she looked like she was out. Once I got to the bridge, I pulled the jeep over to the shoulder and got out. I fingered the glass shard in my pocket and walked back to look at Sonny.

"*Hard times, hard times,*" the demon said. "*Hard times. Killing time.*"

Feeling a push that bumped me forward, I wrapped my free hand around the woman's mouth and jabbed the glass into her jugular and cut downward. Her eyes flew open, looking into mine, as she struggled. Her whine was slipping through my hand. I pressed it tighter across her mouth. Sonny stirred as she struggled. Fearing that she would wake him, I got a handful of her hair, still holding the shard in my hand, and yanked her out of the jeep. She was losing strength now. I drug her to the edge of the bridge, lifted her up to the railing, and pushed her into the bayou below.

This was getting easier, but something still bothered me. As I neared the sleeping Sonny Nolans, I caught myself humming "Wagon Wheel," as a way to keep calm. I looked at Sonny's eyelids. I felt breath on my neck. My humming grew louder. With the shard of glass, I stabbed Sonny multiple times in the side of his neck. His eyes opened as well as his mouth, but he didn't scream. Blood was spurting and he couldn't get a hand to his wounds. He tried once, but his hand slipped away due to the blood and I stabbed his reaching hand for good measure. The

49

stabbing felt good, surprisingly. That tight pressure just as the shard punctured the skin and then the release as the shard came out.

Sonny's eyes rolled over and looked at me, utterly amazed and terrified, then the lids closed and Sonny slumped forward.

I pulled him from the jeep and drug him across the bridge. No way I was going to dare go down to the bayou below, but I wanted to have Sonny close so I could drop him over once I got his hand. I snapped and twisted Sonny's left hand, getting it loose enough to twist 360 degrees. It was harder work than I thought it would be. I had to use the glass shard to cut into the flesh and sever some tendons. It cut my hands up a bit too. More pressure was needed, so I placed Sonny's arm under the railing and jerked it up. Finally it ripped free, taking some bone with it from below the wrist.

Next came the other hand. It didn't take as long to get it off, but it was still hard work. I was sweating, so much so that I had soaked my shirt, and my heart was beating faster than a March hare's.

"Sloppy! But done!" The voice shouted. "Got some o' Sonny's blood on you. Bes' be careful where you go tonight. Gone have to get clean soon's you can."

I stood by the jeep and watched the two inside. They were out of it, likely to not wake up until noon. As I watched them, I debated on what to do next. I leaned into the back, trying to avoid getting more blood on me, and took my guitar case out, laid it on the asphalt, and opened it. I took out the guitar and opened my pick compartment inside the case. It was big enough for the two hands to fit, so I packed them in tight and closed the compartment and placed my guitar back inside and sealed the case.

This is really going to put a damper on their tour, I thought. Then I pondered what my step or steps should be. I decided to move the jeep, so I put my guitar in the back and went to Sonny's mutilated corpse and removed his shirt and then dropped his body into the bayou. I heard a sickly smack as Sonny's body hit his girl's in the stagnant water.

I got in the driver's seat and wrapped the shirt around my hands before starting the Wrangler and driving off.

It started to sprinkle and soft claps of thunder rumbled in the distance, followed by wicked smiles of lighting that glowed behind the clouds. It was time to leave the jeep. I drove it off 61 and parked it in the woods and got my gear out of the back.

US-61 was to my left. It would be my silent guide as I walked north.

I was on my feet for about twenty minutes before it started to downpour.

"Hard times, hard times..." the demon mused. "I believes you's heading the wrong way. Ain't gone find no gypsy woman up *north!"* Thunder clapped and enforced the demon's sentence. It made me jump. I actually stopped in my tracks and looked around. Swallowing, I started walking again. The demon's cackling surrounded me. I was soaked, and my pants and shoes were starting to get sloppy with mud.

I reached a railroad crossing where a freight train was heading east. A car carrying a bunch of pipes passed and I chased after it. I grabbed the ladder and climbed on. As I did so, the demon said, "Say, you got a ticket for this ride?" Its mad laughter followed.

The pipes were big enough for me to get into and lay down, so that's what I did.

Chapter 5

I woke, feeling the warm, sultry air of the day. The pipe I was in shaded me from the morning sun, but the light of day kept me awake, even though the slow, rhythmic pull of the train tried to rock me back to sleep.

I slid myself out feet first and sat by the mouth of the pipe. The train was passing through some ramshackle town. A lot of dirt roads and houses that made me think of slave quarters. Everyone I saw had a morose look on their face. *First circle of hell,* I thought.

The train kept a rolling and hit a switch in direction. Instead of east, we were now going south.

Through the foliage, as the train passed a Dollar General Store, I caught a small green sign that said Slaughter.

The train had led me to Slaughter. I gave a half-hearted laugh at that and took it as a bad omen. If it had led me to Slaughter, where else would it lead me?

I got off. Any further south, I'd be back in Baton Rouge.

Cops were probably looking for Sonny, maybe me. So I was cautious about being on the road. *I really need a map,* I thought as I sat watching the rest of the train go by.

When the end car passed me, I stood and followed the tracks I had previously ridden. I was heading north and it bothered me that I was still in Slaughter.

The morning smelled of swamp and there wasn't one close by. As I walked, I realized I was smelling me. I looked at my dirty, stained shirt. It was once light blue, but the years of wear and travel had turned it into a light greenish-gray color. There was also some of Sonny's blood, now dry and brown, that the rain did not wash off.

I took off my damn, stained shirt and put on a western style button up. My old shirt I buried under a railroad tie and then I continued north. The tracks ran parallel to LA-19, what must have been Slaughter's main nerve, and I soon found myself exposed to houses and businesses. The smell of swamp still filled the air. I noticed a gas station with one pump to my right and went inside. I grabbed some water, a couple of protein and granola bars, and a cup of coffee. As I was paying for all this, I asked the clerk if they had maps for sale. He grabbed one from behind the counter and added it to my purchase.

I returned to the tracks, and luckily wasn't exposed for too long. Soon I was enclosed by trees and foliage, LA-19 still to my right but out of sight.

When I finished my coffee, I sat down on the track and looked over my map. The next town north of here was Ethel, and it looked to be smaller than Slaughter. Luckily, I could follow the rails all the way to Ethel and then take 956 southeast to other connecting roadways.

My destination, I decided, was Covington or Hammond, Louisiana. Both were near the coast but Covington looked to be the place I could find a swamp gypsy, some hoodoo that could add Sonny to my Patton/Johnson bone pick.

Near Clinton, around two in the afternoon, I hitched a ride with someone nice enough to give me a lift to Pine Grove. I got a burger there and continued on foot. I thumbed another ride after Pine Grove that was heading to Independence. This one acted a bit nervous around me. Maybe it was the first time he picked up a hitchhiker, or maybe he could smell the carrion from Sonny's hands.

It was four when I was dropped off in Independence.

I reached Hammond by six o'clock and had a bite at a diner while I went over the map. From here, I could take 190 into Covington.

Once in Covington, I hoped to find some superstitious old timers around some of the bars, ones that would know of swamp gypsies or voodoo queens.

Candles were being lit as I entered town. Letting out a soft glow through the windows. It wasn't night yet, but the sun was on its descent. I felt a prickle in the atmosphere around me and knew that my demon was here. "Hmmm," it mused, "me thinks some'in' of 'po'tence happened here."

I walked by a church.

"Ah! Ritual. But for who?"

I didn't respond.

The demon chuckled.

Finding my way down to the river, I saw a post in the ground with pointed signs that read English Tea Room, Barbers and Bombshells, Buster's Place and Oyster Bar, amongst others. The places listed seemed to be too classy for the people I was looking for, but I had to start somewhere.

I went up the street and found the oyster bar and went inside. I should have known from the people smoking outside that the place would be busy. Even so, I managed to squeeze into a spot at the bar between a crowd of obese bikers. Five minutes went by before the bartender came around and asked what I wanted.

"Spiced rum and a lager," I said. "Any kind will do."

He ID'd me and then took care of my order.

After some time went by, I did try and talk to some people. When one of the tenders came by to get me another drink, I asked about the candles being lit.

"Sabine Marcelle was killed," he said.

"Ah. I'm just passing through. Who's Sabine Marcelle? How'd she die?"

"She helped a lotta people. Some think she was murdered, some think she committed suicide. Bled out," he said, and walked away.

I had been about to ask him another question, but he obviously didn't want to hear it. I then went to grab my drink and realized that he had taken my empty glass without taking my order.

Someone was chuckling off to my right. I turned to see a man through the crowd. He was at the end of the bar next to the wall, looking at me. He said something but I couldn't hear him, so I got up and went over.

"Bad business to be talking about Sabine," he said, then he looked past me and said, "Your stuff gonna be okay over there?"

"It's safe."

"Brave."

"What's with Sabine? What's bad to talk about?"

He chuckled some more and took a sip of dark beer. "She was a good person. I 'spect she had a hard past. Sometimes those dark parts don't wash out; they just turn gray on our white souls." Another drink.

I nodded. "Or they grow darker. Anyway, there's got to be more than that."

"Sharp eye, son, sharp eye. But not those; you've got another awareness about you. May be the same that Sabine had. What brings you to Covington?"

"I'm looking to meet someone, maybe a few people."

"Who's the main one you are looking for?"

"The type of person that most people who go to a place like this wouldn't know about. You may know something, though. I get the impression that you know this town well. Is there a bar here on the river, maybe a place where the 'high class' types wouldn't go to?"

He mused and said, "I believe I know a type of place, but what do you seek to find there from a person that you can't find here?"

"Are you a monk or guru?"

"Far from it, but you won't find much in the place I'm thinking of, except less good beer and even less good liquor."

"Well, if I decide I want to get silly, I'll come back here or find another place. What's the name of the bar that's on your mind and where is it?"

He finished his beer. "I'll take you there," he said, and then to one of the bartenders he said, "Slim, cash us out. Got somewhere else to be."

My new friend drove a Chevy truck that was a

55

reminisce of the late sixties. We went over the Bogue Falaya river and went north. I don't know how many roads he took, but most of them were dirt. Finally we came to a stop outside of a place that fit the description of what I was looking for, but it wasn't so unkempt looking. More out of the way than hidden. The name of the place was *Drinkers and Gamblers*. It had a tin roof, a weedy gravel parking area out front, and sat by one of the river runoffs. Vines covered the side of the building like an obsessive woman.

"Lookin' for a gamblin' joint, weren't ya?" he said.

"Something like this."

He killed the engine and leaned over close to look at me. "What are you really after, son?"

Maybe this was the man I had been looking for after all. "I'm looking for a swamp witch, a gypsy, or a voodoo queen that can help me with something."

"Hmmm. And you thought a place like this would have someone who knows what it is you seek? Funny how it all works out. See, some people believe that Miss Sabine Marcelle was murdered by such a person – a witch – though the people of Covington aren't so familiar with that life as you seem to be."

"Do you know of one?"

"Not personally. I know of a place where a friend of mine and maybe some others could help you out. I don't mess with magical stuff. Too many evil forces can get mixed in."

"I'll take my chances."

"Okay, *Wanderer*," he said and started his truck up again. He drove out and we were on our way to another location.

We never crossed into Covington and stayed on the eastern side of the Bogue, going south. Paved roads most of the way, and then he turned off onto a dirt road and then another. The sides of the road were congested by foliage. Through some of it, I could see the stars and moon reflecting off swamp water.

The truck stopped. Through the windshield, I saw that there was a gate, and farther down the road and through the trees I could see electric lights.

"Gate shouldn't be locked, but if it is, then he ain't open," said my friend. He got out of the truck and checked the gate. He looked back at me and smiled as he opened the gate and then got back inside the truck and continued down the road.

The place we pulled up to was exactly the place I was looking for. The only people who would know about this place would be the ones who knew all the secrets of the swamp and the people who wanted to be secluded there.

"Here be the place you're after, I 'spect," he said.

"Yep," I said, as I looked at it. The structure was tall, its timber supports going into the swamp, and long steps leading up to the walk-around deck. Tall trees surrounded the place, their branches and Spanish moss hanging over it like a death veil.

"This place's got some domestic brews, but they ain't got a liquor license, so don't expect any store bought spirits. Luckily they got some swamp rum and moonshine."

"How do they get by with that?" I felt dumb for asking as soon as the question was out of my mouth.

His high pitch laughter filled the cab before he spoke. "Hell, son, ain't nobody know about this place except those who *know* about this place, you see?"

We entered to John Lee Hooker's "I'm Gonna Kill That Woman" playing. There were alcohol advertisements on the walls, some mirrored and some glowing. The majority of which were Budlight.

The bar itself was oval shaped and centered in the middle. This place was out of the way, very secluded, but there were still a good many people here, and despite my shoddy appearance, I felt overdressed.

We approached a less crowded side of the oval bar.

The bartender, an elderly man smoking a corncob pipe, came over. "What'll it be?"

"Some of the spiced stuff," my friend answered.

The bartender looked me over, then went off to take care of the order.

"What's your name?" I asked my new friend.

He chuckled. "I don't have your name either, you know? But I think I know who you are. Believe I've heard a song or two of yours." He chuckled some more and waved it away with his hand before saying, "Call me..." our swamp rum was placed before us, "... Mr. Fiddler."

I picked up my glass. "Are you a musician?" I asked Mr. Fiddler.

He took his glass and said, "Maybe once." He raised his glass and said, "To your health, Bluesman," and we both drank.

I reached into my pack and took out a cigar. I was about to put it into my mouth and then I remembered Mr. Fiddler. "Cigar?" I asked him.

"Maybe later," he said. "Enjoy yourself."

I bit the end off and lit my tip.

On our second drink, I asked Fiddler who I should speak to.

"You asked for a place to find such people. I've led you here. Now, go find those you're looking for."

I took a puff of my cigar and eyed the bartender, who had his back to me. Then my eyes traced the other people here. I decided that the best person to talk to first would be the bartender. So I finished my swamp rum and asked for another. When he brought over another glass I said, "Sir, I'm looking for someone, and I expect you know the type I'm looking for or at least someone else that would."

"Uh-huh?"

"I'm looking for a swamp witch or a voodoo queen. Hell, even a gypsy."

He leaned forward and placed both elbows on his bar, his corncob pipe almost touching my cigar's cherry.

He took the pipe from his mouth and said, "What's your endgame?"

"That's my own business, but I need someone who's practiced in the arts: hoodoo, witchcraft, bone working."

"Jerry James Lou send you here?"

I was shocked by his question and jerked back with an inquiring look on my face. "Guy, I'm new in this place," I said, "I've been all around looking for someone to help me on my task. I don't know a Jerry James Lou. The only one I know in this town is my friend here," I said, as I gestured to Mr. Fiddler.

The bartender leaned in closer. If I didn't know better, I'd say he even took a whiff of me. "Well," he began, "I may know of one, but you'll have a time getting there."

"I would expect nothing less."

The pipe went back in his mouth.

"Look, I'm not broke. If it's a bit of money, I can pay."

"You think money's an issue?"

"I don't know what is. Everybody's looking for something. The price may not be in the value of money, but there's always a price for something."

"Well, I don't have a price for just telling you a location. Getting there may be different."

"Whatever, tell me what you need, and I'll do it."

"I know of such a witch, but I won't take you there."

"How can I get to her?"

"She ain't really wanting to be found."

"Obviously. Look, I'm a person she'll want to see."

"Mhmm. See that boy over there shooting pool?" He gestured to a room off to my right

I looked.

"The one without a hat. Go and speak to him, but best wait until his game is over."

I backed away from the bar and went to the enclosed section with the two pool tables. I leaned against the wall and puffed at my cigar while I sipped my swamp rum. As

I watched the players and the other patrons, a song began to develop in my head, but I would soon forget it.

When their game was over, I went to speak to the man without a hat. "The swamp witch," I said, "I was told you could take me to her. That she can only be reached by boat. If you know the place, will you ferry me?"

"She without a name," he said to me.

I didn't respond.

"Yeah, I can take you to her," he said.

"How soon?" I asked.

"One more game. Let me think about it."

He played his one more game, and after he won it, I continued the conversation.

"If it's a matter of crossing," I said, "don't worry; I can pay her too."

After close to an hour of persuading him, he finally agreed to take me to her for a cigar and two hundred dollars. I agreed and two or three hours later, we were in the swamp on a fiberglass pirogue with a small motor.

As we rode, I felt the demon's presence as well as Blind Willie's "Dark Was the Night." All of it seemed to cloud around me, a charge of energy that filled my nose with ozone.

The motor went quiet. I turned to look at my navigator. The nightlife of the swamp came in over the silence. "Gotta come in silently," said my guide.

"You mean sneak up on a practiced witch?"

He had a push pole in hand and was standing, quietly moving the boat to our destination. "Wouldn't try to sneak up on her," he said. "Matter a fact, I don't know if it can be done, but she'll know you're friendly if you come in gently."

"How far are we from her?"

"A mile, maybe a little more."

"Jesus. You really do have to come in quietly."

Chapter 6

"**H**ow it is," he said, and we didn't speak to one another the rest of the way.

We pushed up on a soggy bank and my guide shined a light to check for dangers. There wasn't so much as a snake, so we got out and pulled the pirogue further ashore. He kept his light out and I followed beside him.

"She won't mind the light?" I asked.

"She knows we're here. Long as I don't shine it in her eyes, she'll be okay with it. I'll switch it off when we get to her."

My guess was that we had landed on an island, and we walked through sedge and amongst tangled branches, then came to a place where the vegetation wasn't so thick, but the ground was muddier.

"Stay behind me," said my guide. "There's quicksand about here." He cast the light beam up into the trees. The closest one was a bald cypress with an alligator pinned high on its trunk. The light moved over to another and shone a human skeleton hanging upside down. "The trees that show the most threatening thing are the safest ways to take."

Once past the quicksand and hidden traps, we came upon a mud hut by what looked to be a small pond. I heard a click and the light went out.

We walked forward, slowly approaching the hut. There weren't any candles lit inside and it looked as if it had been abandoned for quite some time.

"Are you sure she still lives here?" I asked.

Sounding lik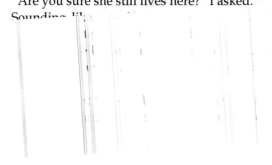

too. Something new to add. You should have told me about the four friends you brought with you.

"Boatman, you can leave us."

"Yes, Madame," he said and hurried away.

"He's my ride," I said dumbly.

"I did not dismiss him from my island; he will still ferry you away, if I allow it." I caught her movement by the stagnant water. She stood and I could see her lean form as she came toward me, but I could not see her features. Finally, she was close enough for me to see her. Her skin was sleek and looked as if she had just crawled out of the mud. She stood face to face with me and looked me over. Despite her appearance, she had a good smell about her. "What have you brought for me?"

I placed my guitar case on the ground and took out the two rotting hands and then showed her the pick. "This is made from the bones of – "

"Robert Johnson and Charlie Patton," she finished for me. "One bone from the left hand and one bone from the right." She looked down at Sonny's rotting pickers. "And now you want more bones to add, to extend your charm. Won't be easy, won't be fast, and it won't be cheap. Ol' Sonny Nolans paid a fine price."

The demon started to speak to me. I could feel its presence and the air change as if it were taking a breath, but she stopped the demon before it could say anything. "Cease your spins, devil. You're not welcome here. I'll have Papa and da Baron take you to that hell you refuse to dwell in!" And like that, the atmosphere returned to normal. The hostile presence gone.

"I'll mend your pick," she said to me at last. "I'll warp Sonny's bones around this," she said and held up my pick. "Go tell your guide that you'll be here awhile, that he should come back in a week's time. Go, chile."

I did as she bid me to do.

Going to my guide and coming back to the hut scared me. I didn't like walking perilous ground with limited sight.

Her hut was still absent of light, but the stars reflecting off the water behind it helped guide me the rest of the way. I knew she was around but there wasn't a sign of her, and my guitar and pack had been moved from where I had left them. They were probably in the hut, but I wasn't going to dare enter it. But peek in?

I neared the entrance and saw my guitar case leaning against a warped dresser inside.

"Can you play without your magic artifact?" her voice asked.

I was silent in thought, then I answered, "I can play, but I can't give it *sound*."

"Ahhh, you've let otherworldly forces guide you, and then you took them for a crutch. In doing so, you've gained something nobody else 'as."

My eyes were transfixed on my guitar case and I remained silent.

"You look at your instrument like a libido lost lover looks at his woman." She laughed and I realized that I had another demon now. "You want to touch 'er, but you know neither one of you will get any pleasure." She laughed again. "What would someone get from you if they decided to carry around part of *your* body as a charm? Would they be lucky? Would you enhance their skill?"

Again, I was quiet.

"Chile, you don't trust me to answer, but enough to work your precious charm and artifact? May be that you too desperate and are forced on faith to bring it to

back of the hut and saw her figure standing waist deep in the water. With my back resting against her hut, I sat watching. She stayed where she was for quite some time, facing me or not, I couldn't tell, but later she slowly descended and did not resurface for me to see.

Next I saw her, she was coming around to sit by me. She was topless except for a necklace of wooden beads and necklaces of ferns. Around her waist was a dripping, tattered loincloth. "Whatcha watching now that I am here?" she asked me as she sat.

I rocked my head in thought and said, "The steam, the night, how calm the water is."

"Peaceful."

I nodded. "How soon will you start on adding more to my charm?" I asked, after a time.

"Already have."

* * *

I don't know when I fell asleep, but that's the last bit of conversation I remembered having. Next I knew, I was waking up beside her inside the hut on a bed of soft, dry grass. My hand immediately went to feel my groin and pubic hair. Nothing felt dry or flaky, and I relaxed, knowing that we didn't do any more than sleep together.

I got out of bed and heard her say, "Fetch breakfast, chile. There's a cage that's got some moccasins. Catch a snake, and I know you've got something special 'bout you."

"Wait, wha—"

"Don't talk; just do as I bid you."

By her hut, near the water, was a chicken wire cage with six or more snakes. They hissed then became defensive as I neared. I lifted the mesh wire top and looked at them. *No way that crazy hoodoo-voodoo woman thinks I'm going to stick my hand in here.*

Still holding the top up, I looked around. There was a maple tree near, so I walked over to it. I looked up at a fresh branch, strong and long enough to use, but it was out of reach and I wasn't about to climb this thing for it, but the ground had several broken branches. I felt along with my foot and found a decent branch and lifted it up with my foot to grab. As I did so, the leaves started to move and I saw a large cottonmouth slither toward me. "Son of a bitch!" I shouted in surprise, and brought my left foot down awkwardly on top of it. The strike was aimed to kill the thing, but all I ended up doing was pissing it off even more. I went to smash its head with the branch and then remembered what Miss Voodoo Queen of the Swamp – or whatever the hell she was – asked of me. So, instead of killing it, I pinned its head with the branch and cautiously grabbed the snake at the base of its skull and picked it up.

I came round to the hut's entrance, still holding the moccasin at the base of its skull.

"What, you don't think snake taste good as breakfast?" was the first thing she said to me. "Don't come bringing that thing in 'ere, get it cookin' and we'll eat."

I could hear her laughing as I walked away. Safely holding the snake to the ground with my left hand, I bashed its skull open with the butt of my branch and went to get a fire going.

It cooked up nicely and made for a good breakfast.

The rest of the day I was alone on the island. My swamp witch disappeared on me sometime after breakfast. Throughout the day I walked the island, trying to get my whereabouts and which routes were safe and which routes were dangerous. On my way back from the

I went to the corn and picked four ears and then grabbed some carrots. I cradled them in my arms as I looked around. If there was anything else I wanted or that she wanted, I would come back with a pail.

There was a wicker basket on a table of warped wood in the hut and I dropped my gathered crops in it and went back outside. I smelled smoke coming from some part of the island. It made me think of grilling and my stomach grumbled. I looked at my resting guitar case and took my guitar out and sat by the hut's entrance and began to play.

Though I was off, even on my own songs, it felt nice to have it back against my chest with my arm around the body and my fingers on the steel strings.

I put it away after about forty minutes to an hour of playing well, but not playing like myself. It was weird but I felt as if I were someone trying to do a cover my own songs.

A shadow fell across me as I clamped the last latch shut. I looked up.

She was back.

"Touchin' her, but you ain't got all your mojo, do you?" she asked, and went inside. Then I heard her say, "Ah, chile, I see you found my garden. Go fetch some more. Get peas. I've already got some green beans. Stringed too. You lucky."

"Do you have a pail?" I asked.

"Come in, you'll find it."

I went back to the garden and I was there for maybe an hour, then it started to rain. Hard. So hard that I could barely see to find my way back. Once, I got lost and about stepped on a trap that would have sprung a spiked monstrosity that would swing down from the tree above. Somehow I made it back safe, and she was waiting for me by the hut's entrance. She stepped aside as I neared, allowing me to enter. I set the pail in the corner and turned around. She stepped near me and handed me a wooden cup. I sniffed the contents. It was rum and not that awful swamp rum I'd had the other day.

I sipped my rum. It was better than I'd expected, so I downed the rest of it. She smiled and went to get a growler from beside her dresser. She poured some more rum and I drank. "This is really good," I said. I looked around the small hut. "I haven't noticed a still or any distilling equipment."

"It's from the mainland," she said, and took a drink of her own. "I do favors for people and then they do something for me." She smiled over her wooden cup and chuckled, then said, "That's why this tastes so good. I think this is Sailor Jerry."

"Well, whatever it is, it's good."

She sat on the bed.

Outside it thundered.

She pat the bed, intending me to sit.

"What's your name?" I asked her.

"Funny that a person would wait so long to get to know another person," she said. "Are you afraid of me?"

I sighed and said, "No. But I'm wary of you, in a way. You could easily kill me, I know you're dangerous, but I haven't given you reason to harm me. In fact, I'd say I'm interesting to you; I've brought you something that's challenging, and you know of my problems and what haunts me – also, my guide here said you have no name."

She laughed and said, "You're open with a stranger, and with a swamp hoodoo, too."

I sat beside her and took a drink. "Not much scares me. There are things I won't do and places I'll avoid, but it's... it's for, I don't know, for self-preservation." I took a my ability, my skill. And then losing someone to offer my services to."

I nodded, thinking, and took a sip.

"And you, Bluesman, what are you afraid of?"

I had another drink and remained quiet. She filled my empty cup and kept the growler nearby.

"Everyone fears something. Keeping quiet won't kill the fear... You don't seem to be afraid of death, but you don't have an excessive life either."

I sighed heavily and said, "I'm not afraid of death; I'm afraid of dying for a long time."

"That's all we do, chile. Spend our days dying. Some faster than others, as Sonny Nolans found out."

"No: anyone who doesn't feel like they're living might as well be dying. Dying because there's no tomorrow, and there is no now."

"And are you living?"

"Yes. Especially when I'm playing."

"How about when you kill?"

I was silent for a long time. Finally I answered. "There's a rush, I won't lie, but I don't want to kill anyone just to kill. Other than Sonny, there were two more. One person I killed in defense. Another I killed because I couldn't chance being identified, and Sonny I killed because I needed his skill to progress mine. He was innocent and I wish he wasn't."

"Was he more talented than you?"

She refilled my cup and I answered. "He was equal. I'm basically a solo act, he was with a band. Nonetheless, he was the talented musician I needed."

"Can you live with it?"

"I have been. If your question was do I feel guilty, I don't. I just wish I hadn't been so friendly with him, that we hadn't blended so well. He was the type of guitarist I could play with every night." I scoffed at what I had just said. "As it turns out, I will be playing with him every night."

She burst out laughing then, even though I didn't mean to make a joke or even be humorous.

"Care if I smoke in here?"

"Go ahead, chile. Though I may need to send for Baron Samedi if you smoke; rum and cigar? It would be rude not to invite him, and I'll need him to complete the charm."

"*Me casa, su casa,*" I said, and got a cigar out. Thanks to the humidity, the cigars hadn't dried.

"That should be my line," she said.

"Someone had to say it," I said, and she snatched the freshly lit cigar from my hand and took a heavy puff.

All I could think of, as she slowly let the smoke out through a small parting of her lips, was that she was in control. And maybe in my face she saw that I knew that.

"You want something from me," I said. "What is it?"

She exhaled a large cloud of smoke and handed my cigar back to me. A wicked smile appeared. "You *are* sharp."

I knew it, I thought.

"Someone like you I could use for a while. Chile, I could use you for life, but I can't keep you."

My head was kind of swimmy, and I was trying to be careful of what I said. "You consider…" I couldn't talk. I was scrambling for words.

"I am Gabriella Martine. Yet the few who know call me Ms. Martine or Queen Martine. You, however, can call me whichever you like." She stood. "But Queen or Ms; you show me the respect I deserve."

"Yes, my Queen," I said, and put the cigar back in my

Shortly after she was gone, I could hear her voice outside at the back of the hut, faint, due to the storm. Soon it was joined by two other voices, males'.

Lighting lit the night and the inside of the hut. Thunder rumbled, and I heard the Baron's laugh. I took a big drink of my rum and felt quite drunk. I wasn't overly worried, but I did have a fear that the queen would bring the Loa that she had summoned inside. She didn't and I passed out from drink.

Chapter 7

Days passed. Time here existed as if it would go on forever; all that changed was day into night. In the day, if I wasn't gathering food or doing something for the Queen, I picked at my guitar, my confidence and skill growing as I did so. I even managed to write a new song, a bluesy rock type, about the swamp and the Swamp Queen.

As day turned to night, we ate, drank rum, and then she would try and summon the Loa. Only once did they not appear.

Then one night she came to me. I was skinning a snake when I felt her presence. I turned and saw her with some small white cylinder between her thumb and first two fingers as she held the object out to me. It took me a second but I then realized that it was a hollowed bone, shaped into a slide for my guitar.

I took it. "Thank you," I said, slipping the slide over my ring finger.

"Made from part of Sonny's arm; it will help you on your way."

"The pick," I said.

"It's on its way. There's that small matter I need, then you can have your pick."

I was about to ask what a swamp witch, voodoo queen, rather, could want or need, but she let me know.

"There's another like me," she said. "This one operates on land, but by the Bogue. Your guide will be back soon. I need you to have him take you to this… charlatan's place. There, you need to kill her." Ms. Martine

"In a way, but you owe *me* something for my work. Helping amongst me island is one thing, but this is another. There's only one queen of this swamp, of this whole area, that people should come to if they need magic work."

I shook my head in bewilderment and said, "Let's eat," and walked away and slapped the snake down on the grate over a pit of burning coals. A few minutes later she came up beside me with a skillet of thinly sliced sweet potatoes and sat them down over the grate.

"Best keep in mind that you owe me, chile. If you leave here without removing a false adversary, you won't make it far before your soul is in my hands, and I'll be holding the door to hell open for you. I want someone who can help me when you're gone." I was listening but more focused on my cooking. She pushed a gun into my hand and said, "Kill her and bring the corpse back to me."

I looked down to see an old six-inch flintlock pistol in my grasp. I brought it up to examine it. "Jesus Christ," I said, "how old is this damn thing? It looks like it's from Civil War times. If I shoot someone with this it's going to kill me too!"

"This pistol has been in my family since 1780. It's killed Red Coats, French, Americans, you name it. And it's loaded. Jus' pull da hamma back and squeeze de trigger. The one at the end of the barrel won't be doing so well, but you'll be jus' fine!"

I put it in my front waistband.

We ate and then I went to wait for my guide. When he returned, I boarded his boat. He poled away from the island and then started the motor when he felt far enough away. "Where to?" he asked.

I sighed and said, "There's another that claims to be magical. Let's head toward there. Do you know who and where she could be?"

He didn't say anything, but the boat sped up. As we went toward our destination, I couldn't picture the person

I was supposed to kill. I'd done enough killing for the dark side of the afterlife. To keep calm, I hummed some of George Harrison's *Dark Horse* stuff. It was enough to mellow me until we bumped into the bank.

I was climbing out, and had my right foot on the damp sand when I turned to look at my guide and said, "No matter what happens or what you hear, keep close to the bank."

I got fully out of the boat and said, "Actually, if you can pull this thing further onto the bank, I could use your help to carry the body down. I shouldn't take long."

The thick, sucking mud made me rush awkwardly up the bank. Some feet up was a small house. The complete opposite of Queen Gabriella's hut. Winded, I made my way to the front door. I swallowed and knocked.

Quiet.

I knocked again.

"One moment," I heard from the other side.

The door opened and a woman of about sixty years stood before me. "Hello," she said.

"Hi."

"What can I help you with? You look awful. Travel far?"

"I'm a traveler, yes, and it's been a long journey."

"Well, come in, I'll get you something to drink and to eat while you tell me what you seek or what you want me to do." She started to walk inside, saying, "Seems like everyone is looking for more than one thing." I followed her and closed the door behind me. To my left was a small kitchen that she entered. I remained standing, examining

I sat on the love seat by the front door. Ahead was a door-less entry way that led to a dark room. Other than it, I figured that there were one or two more rooms to the place.

Footsteps on linoleum became quiet and I looked to the kitchen. The woman was coming toward me with a glass in her hand. The contents within were brown amongst cloudy ice. "Tea?" I asked her.

"Yes," she said. "Sweet too. It will help you feel better."

"Thanks," I said, and took the glass. I took a sip. Having something cool to drink after not having the luxury for a while did pick me up.

She smiled and returned to the kitchen.

I felt Gabriella's pistol hilt through my shirt. If this woman had any magical ability, I would need to be fast.

She came back with a plate of food and placed it before me on her coffee table. On the plate was fried chicken with mashed potatoes and crawfish. It looked good but I wasn't hungry. She sat in the rocking chair across from me. "So, where are you from?" she began, and then added, "Oh, please do eat, you look famished."

I managed a bite of chicken and then said, "I'm from all over."

"What brings you here?"

I began to speak but a knock came from the door. We both looked at it. There was another knock, and she stood up and started to make her way to the door. Then came another knock, much louder, and I heard the distinct voice of my guide say, "Hey, man, you take care of that yet?"

The woman slowed in her approach. I acted before she could turn to look at me, charging and pushing her into the wall by the door. Hands on her shoulders, I slammed her back and forth against the wall, causing her head to whip against it. I took my right hand off her shoulder and went for the pistol. My fingers felt it and began to wrap around the hilt, but as I was taking the pistol from my waistband, I felt a sharp pain in my left side below my ribs. I looked at the woman. She had a wicked look on her face and the pain began to spread to my tummy.

I pushed her back against the wall and myself away. I looked at where I felt the pain and realized she had stabbed me with a hidden blade.

"You okay in there?" My guide called through the door. "What's going on?"

She began to come forward.

"OPEN THE DOOR!" I shouted. "HARD!" The yelling hurt and I fell to my knees just as the door opened, whacking the woman in the face. She dropped like a rag doll and rolled around on the ground.

"Jesus Christ!" my guide said.

Blood was soaking my shirt and my pants. I fell forward, banging my head, but I didn't lose consciousness. I started to pull myself toward the dazed woman. When I got to her, I got on my knees and turned her onto her back and pressed the pistol against her breast plate over her heart and cocked the hammer and pulled the trigger. The shot was slightly muffled due to the barrel being pressed so hard into her shirt. I started to stand but fell back, hitting the coffee table and pushing it away to where I lay on the floor, staring at the ceiling.

My guide came over and knelt beside me. He lifted my shirt and looked at the wound. "Damn," he said and disappeared. He came back and I felt him putting some kind of cloth on my wound. "Hold that tight," he said. "Got to get some more stuff, but keep that held there." He

"How long was I out for?" I asked.

I had startled him, but he said, "About two hours. I patched you up."

"How?" I asked as I looked at my bandaged side. "Had to be a deep wound."

"It was. I carry a medical suture with me. I sterilized it and stitched you up."

"Why do you carry one on you?"

"Been bit by gators a few times; figured it'd be best if I knew how to stitch a big wound on my own."

I nodded and said, "Smart."

"Take it slow though. You don't want your wound to reopen."

"We've got to get back to the Queen and give her that body."

"Just rest up for another couple hours. If you feel strong enough then, then we can go. But gettin' down that bank with that body is going to be hard enough. Too much exertion and you'll start bleeding again. Too much of that comes undone and you'll bleed out for sure."

"All right."

"And eat a bit of something. You spilt what was on the coffee table, but there's some more in here."

"Sure. I'll have something. That chicken was good. Heat me up a bit and I'll eat it."

I felt better after I ate some more and slept for another couple of hours. When I woke up, I convinced him to help me carry the corpse down. He got a shirt from the woman's room and tossed it to me. It was one of her shirts, light blue, and a bit tight for me, but I threw it on and grabbed Gabriella's pistol and returned it to my waistband, away from my wound.

Getting the body outside wasn't difficult. I felt some strain on my wound, but nothing serious. It wasn't until we started down the bank with uneven steps that I began to feel a lot of pain. I didn't groan, but I was sweating profusely and I was afraid that I was going to start

76

bleeding.

Finally, we got to level ground and the pain wasn't as bad, but the ground was muddy and it would suck my feet. My guide fell once but quickly got to his feet and picked up his end of the body. We got in the boat and he asked me how my wound was. I felt under the shirt around the bandages. "I'm not bleeding, so it's still together."

"Good, good. Think we're good to go then?"

I looked up at the cottage. "Got to do something about her home; a lot of our prints and DNA are there. Best to burn the place. Can you take care of it? I'm not in the best condition to head up there. I'll mind the boat and body."

"Yeah, fine. I'll take care of it," he said and made his way up the bank.

I could tell when he started the fire because the flames flickered off the windows. By the time we were quietly pushing away, smoke was pouring out, and when we were farther out on the water I could see the small house engulfed in flames.

I got really sick on the way back to the island and threw up a lot and even became unconscious. I was woken by Ms. Gabriella. "You did good, chile," she said. "Come. We'll carry the body and you follow behind us, and don't be afraid to lean on me if you have to."

I leaned on her the whole way. They placed the body in a hammock and pulled it high and tied the loose ends of the ropes to stakes in the ground. I stood with one hand on the hut, watching, and feeling as if I were going to pass from my waistband and placed it on her bedside table, then I felt her remove my pants and then my boxers. She grabbed a knife and cut the shirt down the center and then pulled the halves off of me.

Everything she was doing was getting me excited, despite my condition, and within seconds, I felt myself inside her. When I climaxed – when we climaxed – it felt like the best medicine I could ever have, and I immediately fell asleep.

Chapter 8

I awoke, soaked in sweat. It was still night, but Queen Gabriella was not beside me. "My queen," came out of my mouth in a croak. A few minutes later she came in and filled one of her wooden cups with water. She brought the cup to me and I drank the cup dry. It wasn't ice cold but it was cool enough for me.

She grabbed the cup from my hand and filled it once more and handed it back to me. I drank while she watched, shaking her head. When I finished this cup, she said. "I've checked your wound. It's not infected, and I cleaned it once more for good measure."

"More water please."

She obliged me.

"What all happened there?"

"I knocked a few times. She came to the door and asked what I needed and what I wanted from her. Then she saw how worn I looked and invited me in and gave me some tea to drink and a bit to eat."

"Did you have what she prepared?"

"I had a sip of tea and a bite of chicken."

"Poison."

I gasped but then said, "I don't think so. My guide had some of what she had in the kitchen. If there was any poison he would have found it or he'd be going through this too."

"May not be the food, but it has to be poison. Likely, she covered her blade with it."

"Antidote?"

the cup from me and filled it with water and then added some cloudy, light brown liquid to it and swirled the cup and then thrust it at me, saying, "Drink."

I looked into the cup and then at Gabriella.

"Drink," she said.

I did, and coughed multiple times from the bitterness.

She took the empty cup from me and sat it on the stand by the bed and placed the carafe of water beside it.

"What you just drank will help fight the poison," Gabriella said. "You may feel stronger later, but the poison may still linger. When you leave tomorrow, I will give you four vials. Drink one if you feel the pain coming on. Now, you must relax and sleep. I will join you shortly; there is still more that needs to be done."

I lay back down and closed my eyes. I felt Gabriella watching me, then I heard her quietly shuffle off.

* * *

Golden sunlight shone through my eyelids. I opened them to see bits of sunrays coming through Gabriella's tattered curtain. My head was resting on her smooth back. I kissed it. As my lips departed the smooth skin, the back rolled away, bringing up her trim stomach.

I had been nervous about having a sexual encounter with her before, but it seemed that having sex with a voodoo queen was just the medicine I needed.

The air was cool and I was not sweating. I reached down to the floor and grabbed my blood stained boxers and put them on. Next, I slipped on my shoes and went outside. With the help of a thick stick, I snatched up a cotton mouth, crushed its skull with my heel and threw it on the grate. I got some wood and kindling and started a fire underneath. Watching this snake begin to cook, I felt I could eat half of another. The next moccasin I caught I did the same to it as I did the last, but as this one hit the grate, its body started to twitch. It stopped after five minutes, and, with my stick, I turned both snakes onto their uncooked sides.

Gabriella, naked, came to the hut's entrance and watched. I went to her when the snakes were finishing and kissed her and walked by her to get inside. I grabbed the wooden slab I used to put cooked food on and took it out and placed the charred snakes on it and carried the slab over to Gabriella.

We sat against the hut while the snakes cooled.

"Feeling better?" Gabriella asked.

"Yes. Much better." I picked up one of the snakes. It was hot but I was able to pull the charred scales off and then hand it to Gabriella. I watched her take a bite and then I started to clean the scales from my snake.

"I appreciate you preparing the snake to break our fast, but it wasn't necessary this morning, chile." She smiled at me. "I have help on this island now, and she is out there somewhere. Likely in my garden."

"So, you brought her back."

"Enough to help me here. There's not much else she can do."

"I'm sorry."

"For what, chile?" she snapped at me.

"For your help being limited."

"It's always limited in their case. No matter, you did your task. I knew there was more to you than just playing an instrument and using old bones to do so."

I chuckled.

The rest of our breakfast was enjoyed in silence.

I packed everything shortly after. Gabriella was

until my breathing became normal and the spins and nausea stopped.

Feeling better, I got to my feet, slung my pack over my shoulder, and picked up my guitar case. I walked out and looked around for Gabriella. I didn't see her, so I went around back. She was kneeling by the water. I approached and she turned and stood.

When I was a foot or less from her, she extended her right hand, holding the slightly larger pick.

I took it.

"Now, go, Bluesman. Set out and do what you've been trying to do for so long."

"Thank you, my Queen."

She smiled. "Always glad to assist."

I stepped in to kiss her, but she turned her head away and said, "You can kiss me when you return. Until then, remember last night."

I nodded and turned to walk away. I was rounding her hut when she called to me, "And Bluesman, next time you find yourself on this side of Louisiana, be sure to come see me. Even if all you need are my breasts to rest your weary head."

I turned, about to say farewell, but instead, did an old fashioned bow and then made my way to the other side of the island where my guide was waiting. I got in the pirogue and he began to pole us away. As we slowly moved up the Bogue, I turned the pick over in my hand, feeling its smoothness and refined power pulsing through me.

"Any place you have in mind to head to?" my guide asked, sitting down to start the motor.

"How far are you willing to go? I'd like to get out of Louisiana."

"Well, I won't be taking you out of ol' Louie. Still got quite a distance to go north or east to get out of 'er. We'll head a ways northwest though; let you out near Folsom. You got a map?"

"Yeah, I've got one."

Right, you'll do fine then." He started the motor and we sped away until my guide was ready to let me out.

***

The pirogue bumped into a weedy bank on the western side of the river. "Head west from here and you'll get onto the main road," said my guide.

"What road?" I asked.

"Eh… I think it's Louisiana 25."

I shook my head. "How far outside Folsom am I from here?"

"About fifteen miles, give or take."

I rolled my eyes and stepped out of the pirogue, grabbing my pack and guitar case. "Thanks for all your help," I said.

He didn't respond, only pushed away from the bank and turned his boat around and then roared away. I watched him go, growing smaller the farther he got, and then I went up the bank and walked through shin high grass to the road. My guide was right: it was Louisiana Highway 25.

I began my journey northward, which turned out to be a lot of walking and very little rides. Not a single ride until five or six days later, when I was in McComb, Mississippi. A man heading to Jackson was gracious enough to let me ride along with him.

I was still getting sick too, and I only had a fourth a vial left of what Queen Gabriella had given me for the me. The first one offered me a contract the moment he met me, said he had been waiting two years for me to show up to where he could actually hear *me* play. "Fancy slide guitar playing, too," he finally added to his pitch.

The second producer I took up. No contract going in to record the first album. It was something he said we'd talk about as we were finishing up our first recording. Something about this producer seemed right, so I agreed to make a record.

"All right, well, get your things," he said. "We'll be heading to Memphis tonight, start recording the day after tomorrow."

I was at a loss for words at that moment. Then I smiled and said, "Okay. I don't have much, all that you see with me here, but okay."

"Let's go."

We stopped by the club manager on the way out and I got my pay, then we were out the door. He drove a black Buick and he opened the back door for me to drop my pack and guitar on the backseat. Then I got up front beside my producer and we were off, soon to be on I-55, heading to Memphis.

The producer started making phone calls as he drove. The first call was for a hotel for me to stay while I was in Memphis. Then several other calls followed, likely the production manager and a few musicians; I can't say for sure because I tuned him out and dozed along the way.

Recording started the day he said it would. Early too, for me anyway, and we stayed late. I actually slept there in the studio the first few nights.

The recording was supposed to be done as fast as possible because, I'm told, there was such a high demand for an album of mine. I think we stretched the recording time out further than they had planned, but I also started getting sweats and then pains in my stomach. I waited out as long as possible before I drank the remaining concoction in the vial. It had become so bad that I spent hours of recording time in the studio's restroom hugging a toilet. One night I decided that enough was enough, and that if I was going to pass this poison and manage to make music, I'd need what remained of Queen Gabriella's remedy. I took it that night in my hotel room, but I was still sick for the next few days, but my symptoms were lessening.

We had six more songs left to record, and within two days, probably fourteen to fifteen hours each, we completed three.

Two more days went by and my sickness returned, but we managed to knock out a song. The third day we took off so I could rest up. That day didn't do anything for me or anyone but take away time.

I came in early the fourth day and recorded three guitar parts on my own. When the other musicians arrived, I stood with the engineers in the mixing room, listening and watching the other musicians play, occasionally directing them in how to play at certain sections of the song.

When they got it right, we breaked for a two-hour lunch. I took a quick lunch and came back to do more work. An engineer let me hear all the material we had recorded up to that point. I did this for over an hour and took a quick fifteen minute breather before the session musicians returned.

I didn't feel too terribly bad, but I had become very light headed and I was sweating profusely.

Once back in my chair with my guitar on my lap, the microphone hanging before me, and the others ready to moment I opened my mouth, I began to heave.

The bassist was quick to act and brought a trashcan over just in time for me to vomit into.

It was another day that recording was up in the air. I stayed in the studio and slept for a few hours and then we picked up where we left off. Despite my state, we did well and managed to just about finish up. One song remained and we were going to knock it out the next day.

That night though, I couldn't eat and I barely slept.

"Me thinkin' you ain't got much time left," the awful voice said.

I shuddered at its sound.

"I's thinkin' you gone see me preeeeetty soon. Yes, suh, pretty soon. Got some things I'm gonna show you, too, if'n you crossover."

I groaned.

The demon must have found that funny because it laughed the laugh only a lunatic or something truly evil could. It said nothing else that night.

Getting about an hour's worth of sleep, I took to the morning and dressed in my ragged plaid shirt and blue jeans. Most mornings I walked with my guitar to the studio. Today I could hardly stand on my own. I called the producer and asked him to drive me to the studio.

As we made the short drive there, he asked if I wanted to take some time off, maybe finish up next week.

I told him that we might as well go ahead and finish it now.

We got to the studio, and my producer had to help me out of the car. He pleaded to help me into the studio, but I wanted to walk in there on my own.

I sat on my chair and plugged my guitar into the amp.

I looked at the Sonny Nolans bone slide on my ring finger of my left hand and felt the Robert Johnson/Charley Patton/Sonny Nolan bone pick between my fingers of my right hand. I rolled the pick around in my hand, feeling its smoothness.

"Are we ready?" An engineer asked from the mixing room.

"As we'll ever be," I said, and counted us in.

We played. Even if I was dying, I always felt the most alive when making music or making love.

The last song we needed we knocked out in about three and a half hours.

Everyone was satisfied. The session players were mingling and the engineers and sound guys behind the glass were smiling and conversing. I, however, had no strength to stand. So, I said, "Hey, guys, care if I do one more song? Just me alone?"

An engineer pressed a switch on his end, allowing me to hear him as he said, "Yeah, sure. Hey, guys, why don't you clear out to let 'im do his thing."

They left and I sat in silence for a few minutes, listening to nothing.

"Okay," came the engineer's voice, "we're rolling."

I started to play.

When I sang my last note and hit my last chord, I listened to them; the chord growing thinner and my ears straining to hold onto it.

My body drifted to the right. I held onto my pick and kept my fingers clamped on the final chord, ears still straining to hear it even as I slumped dead on the floor.

Christopher S. Allen was born on April 22, 1991. He is a graduate of Concord University and he currently lives in Nutter Fort, West Virginia. Christopher S. Allen began writing novels and short stories for publication at the age of 18 and received his first publication at the age of 21. On the days he is not writing, you can either find him fly fishing, on a cross state adventure, at the pub with a few mates, or simply trying to hone his song writing and guitar playing skills. There are always other projects and undertakings that he is involved with, but he prefers to keep them off the radar until it is time for the reveal.

Follow Christopher at www.kellanpublishing.com and keep up to date with all of his works at Kellan Publishing. Authors love reviews. Please feel free to leave a review for Christopher's "Bluesman" at http://kellanpublishing.com/index.php/authors/authors-c/christopher-s-allen/bluesman-reviews/

Take a look at Christopher's "Outside of Steele," a short horror/thriller story in our horror collection book "Tales of Terror."

Tales of Terror
A collection of horror/terror stories

Outside of Steele
By Christopher S. Allen

Outside the small West Virginia town of Steele, a mutilated body is found sacrificially displayed within a hollow tree trunk. The local police and a detective from the larger town of Phistle begin looking for clues to identify the unknown cadaver and to find out who used him for such a display. What they discover is something far more sinister than they expected.

The Awakening of Samantha Stein
By Richard Phillip Hoffman

In 1983, years before the events of Clan of Midnight, a woman nearing elderly follows the persistent dreams that have haunted her for a half century to a farm in Colorado seeking out the daughter she never had but always wanted who she believes is imprisoned there by some kind of monster. Understanding that, she goes armed, and step by step works her way down through the farm, into a hill, and into the dark to where the girl is and learns more about the girl, the monster, the world she was born into and herself to a far great degree than she could have ever imagined.

Bitch of a Witch
by Boyd Reynolds

Breaking up is hard to do, especially f...

Sabine.Yet there's a twist – should he ever see his ex-girlfriend again, the result will end in murder. He agrees but eventually becomes a pawn between Sabine, Anna and the witch, all vying for power, love and a kiss. On Halloween night, he crosses the border and can't take his eyes off a woman. Finally, he remembers - it's Sabine. The witch's prophecy must be fulfilled, as someone will die at Charlie's hands.

Pick up your copy of Tales of Terror in our bookstore at bookstore.kellanpublishing.com.

Heads or Tails

By Peter Andrew Sacco

There is a serial killer on the loose...maybe more than one! The number of victims is growing as the New Year approaches. The killings are happening on both sides of the USA and Canadian border, and they are different. It appears one of the serial killers is taking sport in "hunting victims" like prized game. The other serial killer has a different method of operation and the signature is very unique--shrunken heads! It is up to former criminal profiler Dr. Thaddeus Michael Thomas to stop the serial killers before he runs the risk of losing his own head!

Get your copy of Heads or Tails at our bookstore at: bookstore.kellanpublishing.com.

Reducing Medical Costs ... at the cost of health
By Reynold Conger

Two members of the Conway family die without a medical explanation. The doctors in the family look into these mysteries and find a conspiracy between Medicare regulators and secondary insurers to shorten the lives of expensive patients.

Now they know too much. They are forced to run for their lives. Can they survive in the mountains? Will justice be done?

Get your copy of Reducing Medical Costs at our bookstore at: bookstore.kellanpublishing.com

CPSIA information can be obtained
at www.ICGtesting.com
Printed in the USA
LVHW081948290620
659290LV00007B/2261